Oliver Optic

Living too Fast

Or, the Confession of a Bank Officer

Oliver Optic

Living too Fast
Or, the Confession of a Bank Officer

ISBN/EAN: 9783337119195

Printed in Europe, USA, Canada, Australia, Japan

Cover: Foto ©Andreas Hilbeck / pixelio.de

More available books at **www.hansebooks.com**

LIVING TOO FAST;

OR,

The Confessions of a Bank Officer,

BY

WILLIAM T. ADAMS,

(Oliver Optic.)

AUTHOR OF "IN DOORS AND OUT," "THE WAY OF THE WORLD,"
"YOUNG AMERICA ABROAD," &C. &C.

ILLUSTRATED.

BOSTON:
LEE AND SHEPARD, PUBLISHERS.
NEW YORK:
CHARLES T. DILLINGHAM,
1876.

PREFACE.

The story contained in this volume records the experience of a bank officer, " living too fast," in the downward career of crime. The writer is entirely willing now to believe that this career ought to have ended in the state prison ; but his work is a story, and he has chosen—perhaps unhappily—to punish the defaulter in another way.   Yet running through the narrative for the sake of the contrast, is the experience of a less showy, but more honest young man than the principal character, who represents the true life the young business man ought to lead.   The author is not afraid that any of his young friends who may read this book will be tempted into an " irregularity " by the example of the delinquent bank officer, for it will be found that his career of crime is full of remorse and positive suffering.

Dorchester, July 1, 1876.

CONTENTS.

CHAPTER I.

GETTING A SITUATION, ... 11

CHAPTER II.

MISS LILIAN OLIPHANT, ... 27

CHAPTER III.

GOING TO HOUSEKEEPING, ... 42

CHAPTER IV.

THE ENGLISH BASEMENT HOUSE, ... 57

CHAPTER V.

LILIAN ASTONISHED — SO AM I, ... 72

CHAPTER VI.

A FAMILY JAR, ... 87

CHAPTER VII.

A Shadow of Suspicion, ... 102

CHAPTER VIII.

Coming to the Point, ... 116

CHAPTER IX.

A Lonely House, ... 131

CHAPTER X.

My Wife and I, ... 145

CHAPTER XI.

Over the Precipice, ... 160

CHAPTER XII.

A Keeper in the House, ... 174

CHAPTER XIII.

The Second Step, . . . , . . 187

CHAPTER XIV.

The House-Warming, ... 156

CHAPTER XV.

My Uncle is Savage, ... 214

CHAPTER XVI.

Cormorin and I, ... 220

CHAPTER XVII.

Providing for the Worst, ... 242

CHAPTER XVIII.

Bustumups at Fifty, ... 256

CHAPTER XIX.

A Crash in Coppers, ... 270

CHAPTER XX.

The Last Step, ... 283

CHAPTER XXI.

An Exile from Home, ... 297

CHAPTER XXII.

Charles Gaspiller, ... 311

CHAPTER XXIII.

My Confession, ... 324

CHAPTER XXIV.

Aunt Rachel's Will, ... 337

LIVING TOO FAST;

OR,

THE CONFESSIONS OF A BANK OFFICER.

————o————

CHAPTER I.

GETTING A SITUATION.

"I DON'T wish to stand in your way, Tom Flynn."

"And I don't wish to stand in your way, Paley Glasswood," replied Tom, with a refreshing promptness, which was intended to assure me, and did assure me, that he was my friend, and that he was unwilling to take any unfair advantage of me.

Tom and myself were applicants for the situation of discount clerk in the Forty-ninth National Bank of Boston. We had submitted our applications separately, and each without the knowledge of the other. If we had taken counsel together before doing so, possibly some sentimental outbreak would have prevented one or the other from placing himself even in a seeming attitude of competition with the other. We had been schoolmates in Springhaven, had been cronies, and agreed as well as boys usually do. It is true he had given me a tremendous thrashing on one occasion, when I ventured to regard myself as physically his equal. Though I could not quite forgive him for the drubbing he gave me, I did, not respect him any the less. While we were good friends, as the world goes, I was sometimes rather annoyed by the consciousness of being slightly his inferior.

Tom was always a little ahead of me in scholarship, and always contrived to come out just in advance of me in every thing in which we were brought into real or fancied rivalry with each other. Still he was never so far before me as to shut me out of the sphere in which he moved. But in spite of my repeated partial defeats, I regarded myself as fully his equal. Perhaps my vanity assured me that I was slightly his superior, for, like the rest of the world, I was human then, as I have unfortunately proved myself to be since. I was tolerably sure that in the great battle of life which all of us are compelled to fight, I should come out all right. When it came to the matter of business, I was confident that I should outstrip him.

Both of us had been graduated at the Springhaven High School, with the highest honors, though as usual Tom was a little higher than myself, for while he received the first diploma, the second was awarded to me. Tom was my friend, and always treated me with the utmost kindness and consideration, but I could not help feeling just a little stung by his superiority; by his continually coming out about half a length ahead of me. Springhaven is not so far from the metropolis of New England as to be regarded as a provincial town; and though engaging in business anywhere except in the great city was not the height of his or my ambition, Tom had gone into a store in his native place, and obtained his earliest knowledge of the ways of the world. But when he was twenty-one he obtained a situation in an office in the city in which he received a salary of six hundred dollars a year.

Again, at this interesting period of life which seems to be the beginning of all things to a young man, Tom was ahead of me, for I had gone to the city as a boy of sixteen, and when I was of age, my employers refused to give me over five hundred a year. Tom had been lucky — this was my view of the case. Tom had blundered into a good situation, and it was no merit of his own. I deserved something better than I had, and it was only the stupid and stingy policy of the firm which had " brought me up " that rendered my position inferior to that of my friend.

I had one advantage over my friendly rival, however, in my own estimation. My character was above suspicion, which could not be said of Tom, though in the city not a word affecting his reputation had ever been breathed, so far as I was aware. At the store in Springhaven where Tom had served two years as a clerk, several sums of money had been missed. There was no proof that Tom took them, but a few people in town knew that he was suspected of the theft, especially as he appeared to be living beyond his income. I do not believe my friend even knew that he was suspected of the theft, but inasmuch as he was the only person besides the two partners who had access to the safe where the money was kept, it seemed probable to Mr. Gorham, the senior member, that he was guilty.

It was a serious matter, and the two partners used every effort to discover the thief. They put decoys in the safe, such as marked bank bills, and resorted to various expedients, but it always happened that none of these traps were ever disturbed. Though various sums mysteriously disappeared, the decoys were never touched. Mr. Gorham declared that Tom was too smart for him, and Mr. Welch, the junior, never said much about the matter. At a convenient time, without stating any reason for the step, Tom was informed that his services were no longer required; that a change in the business rendered them unnecessary. The junior partner retired from the firm, and the senior carried on the store alone.

Mr. Gorham was a relative of my mother, and knowing of my intimacy with Tom, he regarded it as his duty to inform her of the suspicions which he entertained. My mother was shocked and appalled. Tom was the son of one of the best men in the town, and as there was no direct proof of the crime, it was not deemed expedient to say anything about it. Mr. Gorham did not say anything, except to my mother, and she, appreciating the kindness of her kinsman, faithfully promised to keep the momentous secret. Probably there were not a half dozen persons in Springhaven who knew that Tom left his place under suspicion, and those were the family and intimate friends of the storekeeper.

I will not say that the knowledge of this circumstance afforded me any satisfaction, but it helped me to feel that I was the superior of Tom; that in being honest I had a decided advantage over him. I could not disbelieve the story as it came from the lips of my mother, though it was possible there was some mistake. Within three years after the change in the firm of Gorham & Welch, the junior partner "went to destruction," and in the light of this after revelation, it was possible that he had appropriated the money. Mr. Gorham hinted as much to my mother, and she, knowing that Tom and myself were still intimate, gave me the suggestion as a confirmation of what I had always said in his defence. I had found it quite impossible to dissolve my relations with Tom, strongly as my mother desired it. Without exactly believing that he was guilty of the whispered iniquity, I felt that he would be a sufferer on account of it.

The position in the bank for which we were both applicants, was considered a remarkably good one for a young man like Tom or me. I had considerable influence which I could bring to bear upon the directors, and so had my friend, but it seemed to be an even thing between him and me. In the light of past experience, I felt that Tom would get ahead of me again, and I was intensely anxious to succeed, in order that I might regain the ground I had continually lost.

I have called my book " Confessions." I mean that they shall be such; and of course I do not set myself up as a model man. I did wrong, and that was the source of all my misery. I shall not, therefore, deem it necessary to apologize for each individual fault of which I was guilty. My readers can blame me as they will—and I deserve the severest censure. I have sent grief and dismay into the bosoms of my friends, and my story is a warning voice to all who are disposed to yield to the temptations which beset every man in his business relations.

I met Tom Flynn on the street, and I think he
2

was sincerely desirous not to step into my path. I am confident he had a genuine regard for me, and that, if he could have been sure of securing the situation in the bank to me by withdrawing from the competition himself, he would have done so on the moment. But there were other applicants, and if he retired from the field at all, he was as likely to do it in favor of some stranger as of me.

"I should like the place, Tom, though I don't wish to stand in your way," I added; but in saying so, I am afraid I only indulged in a conventional form of speech, desiring only to appear to be as generous and self-sacrificing as he was.

"Of course it is my duty to do as well as I can for myself, but if I can get out of your way without losing the chance for one of us, I will do so."

"Thank you, Tom. That's handsome, and I would do as much for you; but as neither of us can foresee the issue, we will each do the best he can to get the place. That's fair."

"Certainly it is; and whichever is successful, there shall be no hard feelings on the part of the other."

At that moment Tom raised his hat to a lady,

and turning from me spoke to her. She was a beautiful creature, and though it would have been quite proper for me to terminate the interview, I was not inclined to do so, for the lady filled my eye, and I could not help looking at her.

"Be sure and come, Mr. Flynn, said she."

"I shall certainly go if nothing unforeseen occurs," replied he. "Miss Oliphant, allow me to make you acquainted with my particular friend, Mr. Paley Glasswood," he added, turning to me.

I was very glad indeed to know her, for I could not remember that any lady had ever before made so captivating an impression upon me, even after a much longer acquaintance. She was not only very pretty, but she was elegantly dressed, and I concluded that she belonged to some "nobby" family. I was pleased with her, and said some of the prettiest things I could invent for the occasion. I hoped we should meet again.

" Mr. Flynn, you must bring your friend with you to-morrow evening," she continued.

" Thank you, Miss Oliphant; I should be delighted to take him with me, and as he is here, he can speak for himself," replied Tom.

" Just a quiet little party of half-a-dozen at our house, to-morrow evening. I hope you will come, Mr. Glasswood," she added.

" I should be very happy to join you, and I will do so," I answered.

She was very pretty, and she seemed to grow prettier every moment that I looked at her. Her eyes sparkled and she smiled so sweetly, that I am forced to acknowledge I experienced a new sensation in her presence. I repeated my promise to join the little party, and no entreaty was necessary to render me a willing follower. She bowed and passed on, mingling with the bright throng that gaily flitted up and down Washington Street. My eyes followed her till she was lost in the crowd, and I almost forgot that I was an applicant for the situation of discount clerk in the Forty-ninth National Bank.

" Well, Paley, they say the place will be filled at the meeting of the directors to-morrow forenoon," said Tom, calling me away from the sea of moonshine in which I was at that moment floating, as my eyes followed the graceful form of Miss Oliphant.

" So I have been told, and we shall have but little time left to work. By the way, who is Miss Oliphant ?"

" She is a very pretty girl," laughed Tom.

" Tell me what I don't know. What is she ?"

" She is the daughter of a small merchant, who is in rather shaky circumstances, they say. He lives on Tremont Street, and has three marriageable daughters."

" If they are all as passable as the one I have just seen, their chances are good."

" I don't know about that," added Tom, laughing. "Miss Lilian dresses magnificently, you perceive; and whoever marries one of those girls will find money a cash article. You shall see them all to-morrow."

" I should say that a wife like this Miss Oliphant was cheap at any price."

" I think so myself, if a fellow can afford such an expensive luxury. But, Paley, we must not waste our time," added Tom, glancing at the Old South clock. " I must find a man who can do a good thing for me at the bank.

" So must I."

We parted, and as I walked down the street, I could not help recalling the vision of loveliness I had beheld in the person of Miss Lilian Oliphant. I was on my way to one of the insurance offices frequented by my uncle, Captain Halliard, a retired shipmaster, who dabbled in stocks, and was a director in the Japan Marine Insurance Company. He had influence, and I relied principally upon him to engineer my application at the bank. He was a man of the world in the broadest sense of the term. He believed in making money, and in getting ahead in business, and though he paid a reasonable respect to conventional forms, I am not quite certain that he believed in anything higher. In character and purposes, he was the very antipode of my mother, whose brother he was.

I found him reading a newspaper in the office. He dropped it when he saw me, and I thought he looked very anxious. He had undertaken to procure me the situation I was ambitious to obtain, and though I don't think he cared much for me individually, he was persistent in carrying out any scheme upon which he had fixed his mind.

" Paley, your chance is small," said he, candidly, after we had passed the time of day.

My heart sank within me.

" I am sorry to hear it," I replied, gloomily.

" Tom Flynn has the inside track."

As usual! It seemed to be laid down as the immutable law of circumstances that Tom should always come out just a little ahead of me. I was vexed. Tom had six hundred dollars a year, while

I had but five hundred. It was cruel and unjust to me. His income was to be doubled, and mine to remain as it was.

"I was afraid Tom would get ahead of me," I added. "But I would rather he should have the place than any other person, if I can't get it."

"Nonsense, Paley. Don't talk bosh! I haven't given up all hope yet, by any means. Tom is well enough, I dare say, but you must have this place, if possible."

"I should like to have it," I added, hopelessly.

"Paley, what was that story about Tom which was kept so still in Springhaven?" continued Captain Halliard in a low tone. "I heard your mother say something about it, when she was speaking about your being intimate with him. I have forgotten about it."

"His employers in Springhaven thought that he took money from the safe."

"Exactly so; that was the idea," added my uncle, rubbing his hands involuntarily.

"But I don't think there was any foundation for the suspicion," I protested, rather faintly, too faintly to produce any decided effect.

"We are not called upon to try the case," he replied, chuckling at his own cunning.

" But I don't wish to have anything to say about that old affair."

" Then you needn't have anything to say about it, except to me. I have begun to manage this business, and I shall finish it."

" I don't want to injure Tom in the estimation of any one," I added.

" Don't be a spooney, Paley. You must look out for your own chances. You can have this place, if we can get Tom off the track."

Although I was not the author of the brilliant idea foreshadowed in my uncle's remarks, I permitted him to develop it. I told him all I knew about Tom's affair with Gorham & Welch. If I stated that those who knew anything about the matter now generally believed that the junior partner was the thief, I stated it so mildly that my uncle took no notice of it. I confess that I virtually assented to his scheme ; at least, I offered no decided opposition to it. I knew that Captain Halliard had only to whisper the fact that Tom had been suspected, and had lost his situation in consequence of this suspicion, to throw my chief competitor out of the field.

Practically, I assented to the scheme ; if I did anything to prevent its being carried into execu-

tion, I only "fastened the door with a boiled car-
rot." I wanted the place, not alone for its emol-
uments, but in order, in the race of life, to sur-
pass my friend. I regard this weak yielding as my
first crime — the crime against my friend, one of
the basest and most loathsome in the calendar of
offences. This was my real fall; and it was
this, it has since seemed to me, which made me
capable of all that followed.

I left my uncle in the office, and went back to
the store in which I was employed. Between the
bright vision of Miss Oliphant's loveliness and the
dark one of my own perfidy, I was nervous and
uneasy all the rest of the day. What was the
use of being over nice? If I did not look out for
myself, no one would look out for me! I think I
did not sleep an hour that night, and the next
day I performed my duties mechanically. About
one o'clock I was rather startled to see Tom
Flynn enter the counting-room.

"Paley, my dear fellow, I congratulate you,"
said he, grasping my hand.

"What's the matter, Tom?" I asked.

"Why, haven't you heard of it?"

"Heard of what?"

"You have been appointed discount clerk in the

Forty-ninth National Bank. 'Pon my soul, I am glad to be the first to tell you of it," added Tom, with enthusiasm, as he rung my hand.

Iniquity had prospered, but only for a time.

CHAPTER II.

MISS LILIAN OLIPHANT.

HOW could I look Tom Flynn in the face, after what I had done, or permitted to be done? He had been my competitor in the race for the situation in the bank, and probably would have obtained it if my uncle had not whispered the old slander in the ears of Mr. Bristlebach, the president. It is true this plan had originated with Captain Halliard, but I consented to it, to say the very least. I could have prevented him from carrying it into operation. I could have protested in the strongest of terms that there was no truth in the story, and that I would not take the place if it were procured for me by such a base sacrifice of honor and integrity. 27

I did not do so. If I protested at all, it was so faintly that my worldly-minded uncle only regarded it as a piece of "buncombe." It is not for me to blame him, for I regard myself as equally guilty of the infamous deed—more guilty, for Tom was my friend. It is a satisfaction for me now to know that I blushed when my old school-fellow entered the counting-room; and to remember that my conscience stung me like a hot iron when he informed me that the situation had been given to me. It was not the glorious triumph which I had anticipated, and I could hardly felicitate myself that I was to step immediately into the enjoyment of a salary of twelve hundred a year. I could not even enjoy the triumph of being, for once, actually ahead of my fortunate friend.

"I congratulate you, Paley, with all my soul," said Tom, with enthusiasm. "I should have liked the place myself, but I am really better satisfied with the result, than I should have been if I had been successful."

"You don't mean that, Tom," I suggested; and I felt that I was almost incapable of giving birth to a lofty emotion.

"'Pon my word, I do, Paley. I was thinking

this forenoon that, if the place fell to me, I should reproach myself for having stood in your way. I never should have felt just right about it. Now I am satisfied—more than satisfied; I am delighted with the result."

"I thank you, Tom. I didn't expect any such magnanimity from any person in this world;" but I comforted myself with the thought that, if the place had been assigned to him, he would have contrived to endure the disappointment which fell to my lot.

"If I had known that you were an applicant, with any chance of success, I would not have entered the field. But it is all right as it is; and I am as much pleased as you are," added Tom.

"I don't exactly see how I happened to get the place," I replied, in order to tempt him to tell what he knew about the canvass, rather than because I was astonished at the result.

"I do," answered Tom, laughing. Your uncle, Captain Halliard, has a great deal of influence with Mr. Bristlebach, the president. Rhodes—you know Rhodes?"

"I know of him; he's book-keeper in the Forty-ninth National."

"Yes; well, he says Captain Halliard had a

long talk with Mr. Bristlebach this forenoon. I have no doubt he made a strong personal appeal for you, and that settled the case."

I should very gladly have believed that I owed my good luck to the personal influence of my uncle, but I was confident that he had used that old slander to procure my appointment. Tom left me after I had promised to meet him at Mr. Oliphant's in the evening. I was sad, and I felt mean. I was tempted to go to Mr. Bristlebach and undo what my uncle had done. I could even procure a letter from Mr. Gorham testifying to the integrity of Tom. Alas! I had not the courage to do justice to my friend. A salary of twelve hundred dollars was too glittering a prize to be thrown away; and after all it was possible that Tom had been guilty — possible, but not at all probable.

Before the store closed I received official notice of my appointment, and informed my employers of my intention to leave them. They did not say much, and I am not sure that they were very sorry to have me go. I went to my boarding-house, and dressed myself with the utmost care for the occasion in the evening. Miss Lilian Oliphant was a bright vision before my eyes. I wondered that she had been condescending enough to notice a person so insignificant as I was. I was thinking only of her, and as the happy moment drew near when I was to see her again, I even forgot my own infamy towards Tom.

Twelve hundred a year! It was an immense sum for a young fellow like me, and with such a foundation for an air-castle, I pictured to myself a pleasant home with Lilian as the presiding genius of the place, shedding unutterable bliss upon my existence. Twelve hundred dollars would hire a house, furnish it, and enables me to live like a lord. If Lilian did dress well, if she was rather extravagant, I could stand the pressure with the magnificent income which would be mine.

I was admitted to the parlor in which the family were seated. Tom and two other gentlemen were there, conversing with the young ladies, all of whom were dressed elegantly, and were evidently "got up" for the purpose of making an impression. Miss Lilian gave me a cordial welcome, and introduced me to the rest of the party. Mr. Oliphant had heard of my good fortune. He congratulated me, and did me the honor to say that I should soon be the cashier of the Forty-ninth National Bank. I was treated with distinguished consideration, and, without exactly knowing why, I felt myself to be the lion of the occasion. Discount clerk of the bank, I was a bigger man than any of the gentlemen present.

Miss Lilian was very gracious to me, but I bore my honors with tolerable meekness. I tried to avoid putting on any airs, and I think I produced a favorable impression. We played whist, and Lilian was my partner; I did not do myself justice, for I was so fascinated by her loveliness that I could not keep my thoughts about me, and Tom and Miss Bertha beat us badly. But Miss Lilian attributed our misfortune to ill-luck, and smiled as sweetly as ever. I may as well hasten to the catastrophe, and declare at once that I was deeply and irretrievably smitten, as I had intended to be from the first. She was very kind to me, and seemed to look with a favorable eye upon me; but I could not, of course, know whether she would accept me. I was fearful that she would require even a bigger man than the discount clerk of the Forty-ninth National Bank.

I left the house at eleven o'clock with the most intense regret. I knew not how soon I might see her again, but I ascertained where she went to church, and I went there the very next Sunday.

It was cloudy, and she did not appear. I was sad and impatient. It seemed to me that I must see her again soon, or I should do some desperate deed. I tried to invent an excuse for calling at her father's house on Sunday evening, but my ingenuity failed me. I dropped in upon Tom Flynn, and talked of nothing but Lilian Oliphant. I hoped he would take the hint, and propose to call upon her that evening, but he would not; in fact, he was going to a prayer-meeting, and only invited me to go there with him. It was not Lilian's church, and I did not wish to go. It would be pleasanter to walk on the Common and think of her, if I could not see her.

I did not sleep half an hour that night. I was madly, desperately in love with Lilian, and I was afraid that some young fellow with only a thousand a year might snap her up while I was waiting to go through all the forms of society in decent and conventional order. I was not to take my desk in the bank till the first day of the new year, a week hence, and I induced my employers to let me off from the last four days' service, for the reason that I was so infatuated with Miss Lilian I could not do anything. I walked by Mr. Oliphant's house twenty times a day, but I had not

2

the pluck to call. On Tuesday afternoon I sent her a beautiful bouquet labelled " In memory of a pleasant evening. P. G." When I had done so, I happened to think that one of my companions during the pleasant evening alluded to was Paul Grahame. It was an awful blunder on my part, for how could she know whether Paul Grahame or Paley Glasswood was the sender of the flowers, which had cost me five dollars! If Paul, who was more intimate in the family than I, should happen to call during the week, Lilian, under the consciousness that such a pretty bouquet could come only from a sincere admirer, might speak a gentle word or bestow a loving smile upon him, which would forever darken my hopes.

The situation looked desperate, and I must call on Wednesday, or drown myself in the icy waters off Long Wharf on Thursday. Water below a reasonable temperature was particularly repugnant to me, and I did not relish the alternative. I wondered if she would be glad to see me. I tried to determine whether her gracious demeanor towards me during that important evening had been dictated by mere politeness, or by a genuine interest in me. I was vain enough to flatter myself that I had made an impression upon her gushing heart. In my native town I had been accounted a good-looking fellow, as revealed to me through sundry "compliments." I thought I was not bad looking, and I consulted my mirror on this momentous question. The result was satisfactory, and I was quite willing to believe that Miss Lilian ought to be pardoned for feeling an interest in me.

On Wednesday afternoon I walked by her father's house seven times, and probably I should have passed it seven times more, if on the eighth I had not seen Lilian at the window. The stars favored me. The dear divinity saw me; she smiled, she bowed to me, and I thought she blushed. Whether she did or not, I blushed, and the die was cast. The thrilling glance the fair being bestowed upon me inspired me with a resolution equal to the occasion. I rushed to the door, and before I had time to change my purpose, I rang the bell.

I was admitted. I asked for Miss Lilian Oliphant, and was shown into the parlor in which she was seated. My heart throbbed like the beatings of the ocean in a tempest, and my face felt as if a blast of fire had swept over it; but I survived. I was more than fascinated; I was infatuated with the fair being before me. I am free to say that no such vision of loveliness was ever realized before or since in my experience.

" This is a very unexpected pleasure, Mr. Glasswood," said she, more self-possessed than I was.

"I beg your pardon for calling," I stammered.

"I'm sure you needn't do that, for I'm very glad to see you, sir," she replied, kindly helping me out.

" I didn't — really — I thought — it's a beautiful day, Miss Oliphant."

"Splendid day!" laughed she; but I saw that she was beginning to be embarrassed.

I ventured to hint that I had spent a very pleasant evening at her house on the preceding Friday; and she was kind enough to say she had enjoyed it very much, and hoped I would call again soon with my friend, Tom Flynn, and have another game of whist.

" I played so badly then that I shall hardly dare to try again," I replied. I was—really, I was — "

" What?" she asked, when I broke down completely.

" I was going to say that I usually play better, but something disturbed me that evening so that

I was not myself;" and I fixed my loving gaze upon the threadbare carpet at my feet.

" Why, what was the matter with you?" laughed the vision of loveliness before me.

" I don't know, but I didn't seem to have the command of my faculties."

" Then you must come again and redeem your reputation, if you feel that you did not do yourself justice."

" Thank you! When shall I come?" I asked eagerly.

" As soon as you please."

" If it were as soon as I pleased, it would be this very evening," I added with a boldness which absolutely confounded me.

" Do come this evening then. We can make up a set without any other help."

Why didn't she say something about that bouquet, and thus enable me to advance a step nearer to the conquest. She did not, and I was afraid the five dollar trifle had been placed to the credit of Paul Grahame. I went away, but I hastened to the florist's and bought another bouquet—price seven dollars. On the card I wrote, " In memory of a pleasant call. P. G*******d." She could not make Grahame out of that.

Early in the evening I rang the bell, and was ushered into the parlor. On the piano was my bouquet, and near it stood Lilian, who, as I entered the room, was in the act of inhaling its fragrance. I think she blushed a little when she saw me.

" What a beautiful bouquet!" she exclaimed with rapture, after the preliminary formalities had been disposed of. " I am very grateful to you Mr. Glasswood, for this kind remembrancer."

" O, not at all; it was the best I could find, but it is altogether unworthy."

" Why, it is positively lovely! It is beautiful, delicious. My friends are very kind. It was only the other day that Mr. Grahame sent me one, but it was not so pretty as this one."

" Did he, indeed?" I asked.

" How stupid I am! Why it was you Mr. Glasswood. I interpreted the initials as those of his name."

Miss Lilian looked upon the floor, and her chest heaved with emotion that agitated me more than her. I fancied it was all right—and it was. I played whist, and the old gentleman and one of the other daughters beat us worse than before. I trumped my partner's tricks, and put my ace upon

her king. But I consoled myself with the reflection that she must be thinking of something
else, or she would not so often have played the
king before the ace was out. We played a double
game, of which whist was the less important;
but we played into each other's hands, and won
the game in which hearts were trumps, if we lost
on all other suits.

I ought to have gone home at ten o'clock, but
I staid till half-past eleven. I was cordially invited to come again, and I may say I went again,
until my visits included every evening in the
week, not excepting Saturday and Sunday, when
all but " fiddlers and fools " stay at home. Before the snows melted we were engaged.

On the first day of the new year I took my
place in the bank. It looked to me then like a
bed of roses; I have since found it to be a bed of
thorns; though I ought to add that I made it so
myself. I knew the routine of bank business tolerably well, though I had much to learn. I tried
to discharge my duties faithfully, and though Mr.
Bristlebach, the president, was a hard man, I won
even his approval. I need not dwell on this season of happiness, for as I look back upon it, I
appreciate it; I could not then.

My services were so satisfactory that when our paying teller was promoted to a higher place in another institution, I was advanced to his situation with a salary of eighteen hundred dollars, and a promise of an additional two hundred if I proved to be competent to discharge the duties of the office.   My uncle and others were my bondsmen.   Never did a young man look forward to a brighter future than I did. .

Every evening in the week I went to Mr. Oliphant's and was treated as one of the family. During the year I had been paying assiduous court to my beautiful charmer. I spent all my salary, and more than all, for I was in debt at the end of this time. I wore good clothes, for I wished Lilian to be proud of me; I sent her bouquets, I took her to the theatre, the opera, the concerts, and to balls and parties, a single one of which in some instances, spoiled a twenty dollar bill. I took her out to ride, and paid for many costly suppers. But Lilian appeared to love me with all her soul, and I was satisfied.

I had found the end of my twelve hundred dollars so easily that I dared not think of getting married; but my promotion decided me. Lilian offered no unreasonable objections, neither did her parents, and the happy day was fixed. - Tom Flynn, who had taken my place as discount clerk in the Forty-ninth National, was to stand up with me. Somewhat oddly, as it seemed to me, my good friend advised me not to marry, and we almost quarrelled over some plain talking which he did. The die was cast; I would not have retreated if I could..

CHAPTER III.

GOING TO HOUSEKEEPING.

I was married in the spring, and the bank gave me my vacation on the joyous occasion, so that I was enabled to make a bridal tour of ten days to the South. I went to Philadelphia, Baltimore and Washington, and while I distinctly recollect that I enjoyed myself exceedingly, and traveled like a prince, I can more vividly recall the rapidity with which my funds were expended. It had cost me all my salary to pay my board and to take Miss Lilian to the opera and the balls, but I could not afford to deprive Mrs. Glasswood of any luxury.

Before we started I was "hard up," and I tried to contrive some clever expedient by which the bridal tour might be dispensed with. I suggested to Lilian that the journey was not absolutely necessary; that some very "nobby" people staid at home after they were married. Her chin dropped down as though a ten pound weight had been attached to it, and she looked so sad and gloomy that I could not think for a moment longer of depriving her of this triumphal march, for so I am afraid she regarded it. Of course I did not hint to her that I could not afford to spend two or three hundred dollars in travelling, for we were still lovingly cheating each other into the belief that she was a princess and I was a representative of Crœsus himself.

There was not a dollar to my credit at the bank, and I had not a dollar to my credit anywhere else. I was fretful one day, and unguardedly mentioned to Tom Flynn that I was short. The generous fellow promptly offered to lend me a hundred dollars. I am surprised now that I was able to accept it, but I did, and he put my "value received" into his wallet as choicely as though it had been as good as the gold itself. But a hundred dollars, though Tom seemed to think it would pay for every thing which it could possibly enter into the head of a groom to procure, was expended in trifles and before we were ready to start upon the bridal tour I was penniless again.

I wanted three hundred dollars, for it would not be safe to start on a ten-days' trip attended by such a helpmate as Lilian with less than this sum in my pocket. First class hotels, private parlors, carriages, the opera in New York, would make large demands upon my purse. I was rather sorry that Tom Flynn had offered to lend me a hundred dollars, for if he had not done so I should have asked him to favor me with the loan I now needed. I could not ask him, after what he had done. My uncle, Captain Halliard was a rich man, though he was a calculating and a careful one. I had been a favorite of his in my earlier years, and I knew that he had a great deal of regard for the honor of the family. I had hardly seen him since he helped me into my situation, for he had been on a business mission to Europe.

Three hundred dollars was nothing to a man of his resources, and, with some sacrifice of pride on my part, I made up my mind to wait upon him with my request. He would understand the case, and readily see that a young man about to be married must incur a great many extraordinary expenses, and it would not be at all strange that he was temporarily " short. " I found the worthy old gentleman in the insurance office, up to his eyes in the news of the day. I talked with him for some time about indifferent topics, about my

I CALL UPON MY UNCLE. Page 45.

mother's health and the affairs of Springhaven. Then I rose to depart, in the most natural manner in the world though I was rather grieved to see that he was not sorry to have me go ; in fact, he returned to his newspaper with an eagerness which seemed to intimate that I had bored him. I took a few steps towards the door, and then, as though I had forgotten something, I hastily retraced my steps.

"By the way, uncle—I'm sorry to trouble you, but—could you lend me three hundred dollars for a few weeks?"

"Three hundred dollars!" exclaimed the venerable seeker after the main chance, just as though I had attacked him in the tenderest part of his being.

"The fact is, uncle, getting married in these times is an expensive luxury, and I find myself a little short, though, of course, I shall be all right as soon as I get settled down."

"It's rather a bad sign for a young man to have to borrow money to get married with," he added with a glance of severe dignity at me.

"Never mind it, uncle. I won't trouble you, then, if it is not convenient," I replied, in a thoroughly off-hand manner, as though the little favor I asked was of more consequence to him than to me. "I shall expect to see you at the house of Mr. Oliphant at the ceremony, and remember the levee is at eight o'clock. Don't fail to be there, uncle."

"Stop a minute! I suppose if you need three hundred dollars, I can let you have it," he added.

"O, it is of no consequence. Don't trouble yourself. Two or three of my friends wanted to lend it to me, but I did not exactly like to accept such a favor outside of the family. Aunt Rachel, I dare say, will be glad to accommodate me."

"Write a note," said he, rather crustily, as he went to one of the desks, and drew a check for the amount I required.

I could not help smiling, as I wrote the due bill, to think of the address with which I had managed my case. I am confident if I had whined and begged until the sun went down, he would have been hard enough to refuse me. Possibly he did not like to have me apply to Aunt Rachel. She was a maiden sister of my father who had about twenty thousand dollars and lived with my mother. Her inheritance had been the same as my father's, but, having no expenses, she had kept certain lands in the middle of the town till they

increased in value so that she was made independ-
ent. As I wished to be her heir, I had always
treated her with the utmost consideration. Captain Halliard managed some stocks for her, and he
was anxious to keep in her good graces.

I put the check in my pocket with the utmost
nonchalance, and again begging my uncle not to
fail to be present at the ceremony, I left him.
It was all right with me for the present. When
I started on my bridal tour I owed about six hundred dollars, which I calculated that I could
easily pay off in six months with my increased
salary. When we returned from Washington I
had barely money enough left to pay the hackman for conveying us to the house of my wife's
father. If I had not been so cautious as to count
up my money, and estimate the expenses of the
return trip, I should have exhausted my exchequer
before we reached home. When I found I had
just enough left to pay these expenses, I told
Lilian that I had received a letter which compelled me to return immediately, though we had
intended to stay two days longer.

She pouted, but I told her I should lose my
situation if I did not go back. She thought I
might get another situation rather than break up

the pleasant excursion so abruptly. I told her I could easily get another situation, but it was not exactly prudent to give up one until the other was obtained. It almost broke my heart to cross her in anything, and if I could have met a friend good-natured enough to lend me a hundred dollars I might have been spared the annoyance. I met no such friend, and we went on cheating each other as before. It was stupid in me to do so, but I had not the courage to tell her that I was not made of money, and I permitted her to believe that my pockets were still well lined.

We returned home, but on the way I was obliged to pretend that I was sick, in order to save the expense of supper aboard the steamer. We had dined at four o'clock, and though it was absurd to eat again at six, Lilian wanted to see who were at the tables; but my pretended illness saved me, and, what was more important, saved the two dollars for the hack hire in Boston.

"What shall we do when we get home?" asked Lilian, as we sat that evening in the cabin of the steamer.

"We shall live on love for years to come," I replied, with enthusiasm.

"Of course we shall do that," she added; but

I thought she did not seem to be exactly pleased with the diet. "Shall we board or keep house?"

"Which do you prefer, my dear Lilian?" I asked, for though we had discussed this question before, she had not been able to make up her mind.

"If we can board at the Revere House, or at Mrs. Peecksmith's in Beacon street, I would rather board."

"It would not be possible to obtain such rooms as would suit us at the Revere House at this season of the year; and I heard a gentleman in Washington say that Mrs. Peecksmith had not a single apartment unoccupied."

"How provoking!"

It was provoking, but I had to invent my excuses as I went along. I did not venture to suggest that my entire salary would not pay the expenses of boarding at either of the places she named. I was too weak and vain to tell her the truth. I deceived her. She had no knowledge of the world, no experience of the value of money, for her poor father had actually ruined himself in a vain attempt to keep up the style of living he had enjoyed in more prosperous days. Nearly all his profits went upon the backs of his daughters,

4

each of whom had been taught to believe that a husband, when interpreted, was money. I did nothing to disturb the illusion.

"I think we must find a place to board for a few weeks, till we can get a house, and then we will go to housekeeping," I suggested.

"We must go to housekeeping if we can't get rooms at the Revere, or at Mrs. Peecksmith's," added Lilian. "But dear ma will take us to board for a time; and really I could not think of going anywhere else."

We went to "dear ma's," and after I had paid the hackman, I had just twenty-five cents left in my pocket. "Dear ma" was willing to take us to board for a time, under the circumstances, though it would be a great inconvenience to her. She would not think of taking anybody else, though she had plenty of house room. I ventured to hint that, as a prudent man, I should like to know what the terms would be, though really it did not make the least difference to me, in point of fact. "Dear ma" did not like to speak of such things; she was going to take us simply as a matter of accommodation — "under the circumstances."

" Of course, Mrs. Oliphant, I understand you, and I am very grateful for the sacrifice you propose to make; but it is always well to have things clearly set forth," I replied, mildly.

"Certainly it is. I always believe in having things in black and white. I suppose it would cost you fifty dollars a week to board at Mrs. Peecksmith's; but I should not think of charging you that," she continued, with a benevolent smile.

"Gracious! I should hope not," I mentally ejaculated, for at the Beacon Street house the boarders walked on Wilton carpets, looked out through windows decked with velvet draperies, slept upon rosewood bedsteads, and had seven courses at dinner, while Mr. Oliphant's house was an old one, its furniture worn out and dilapidated, its carpets threadbare, and the fare — when they had no extra company — below thé grade of a cheap boarding-house. If I had not loved Lilian with all my soul, I should have deemed it a charity to take her off her parents' hands. As it was, she was cheap at any price.

"Whatever you say will be all right," I replied. "I am getting a handsome salary now, and I am willing to pay a fair price."

"I think thirty dollars a week would be no more than the cost to us. Of course I don't expect you to pay anything near what it would cost at Mrs. Peecksmith's."

Whew! I could board at a house only one grade below Beacon Street for twenty. I expected she would say ten, or at the most fifteen dollars, but, poor "dear ma!" I suppose she needed the money to deck out the next daughter for the sacrifice. I could not object. It was all in the family; but I determined to find a house with all possible dispatch.

I went to the bank and took my place. I flatter myself that I was smart, for I won the approbation of even Mr. Bristlebach. I made no mistakes. I was not nervous. When I drew my month's salary of one hundred and fifty dollars, all but about twenty dollars of it went into the purse of "dear ma," for board which would have been high at ten dollars a week. Though Lilian complained of the accommodations, she said nothing about housekeeping. I made some inquiries, and found I could board better for half the price I was paying. I then said something about engaging rooms nearer to the bank. My dear wife protested. She could not leave "dear ma's," where she had all the comforts of a home, and was in her own family. I saw that she was a party to the swindle; that "dear ma" had instructed her what to do and what to say.

My home was no home at all, and I was determined to leave it before I had another month's board to pay. To stay any longer would be ruin. My twenty dollars' surplus would pay for only a few concerts and rides, and in less than a fortnight I was penniless again. My debts began to trouble me. One day Captain Halliard wanted to know if he had not lent me three hundred dollars for a few weeks. I assured him he had, and that I intended to pay him in a few days. Tom Flynn hinted that he was short, though he did not directly say he wanted his money. My tailor was becoming slightly unreasonable, and the keeper of a livery stable stupidly insisted upon being paid, and even had the audacity to refuse to trust me for any more teams.

It would not do for me to have these importunate creditors coming into the bank to see me. The president and the cashier would be alarmed if they discovered that the paying teller was in debt. But trying as these duns were, they were insignificant compared with the annoyances which I endured at " dear ma's." Lilian hinted, and then insisted, that I should refurnish our room at my own expense. I told her I would think of it, and went out to walk after dinner. I did think of it; and thought I would not do it. Strange as it may seem, " dear ma " was absolutely becoming disagreeable to me, and I wondered how such an angel as Lilian could have been born of such a designing woman as I found her mother to be.

I stumbled upon a friend who had been to look at a house. It was a splendid little place, but not quite large enough for him, and the rent was only six hundred dollars a year. I went with him to see it. It looked like a fairy palace to me, and was just the size I wanted. It was an English basement house, three stories high. I went to see the owner. Another man had just left it, and meant to take the house, but he must first consult his wife. If I stopped to consult mine, I should lose it, and I closed with him on the instant, regarding myself as the luckiest fellow in the world.

Lilian would be delighted with it; there could be no doubt of that. What a magnificent surprise it would be to her, if I could take her in, after it was all furnished! Stupid as the idea may seem to lady housekeepers, I was so enamored of my plan that I determined to put it into operation. I was satisfied we could live in this gem of a house for less than I paid for board, and live in much better style.

The idea of a surprise to Lilian was delightful to me, and I laid out the plan in detail; but the first thing was to provide the funds. Then my jaw dropped down. I owed over six hundred dollars to certain restless creditors; but I could save money by going to housekeeping, and my duty to them required that I should do so. I had not yet troubled Aunt Rachel, and taking Lilian with me, I went down to Springhaven to spend the Fourth of July, ostensibly to escape the noise and dust of the city, but really to lay siege to my venerable aunt's purse strings.

The only thing that was likely to defeat me was the fact that Aunt Rachel did not like my wife, for Lilian, who regarded the worthy spinster as an " old fuss, " had not always been as prudent in her presence as I could have wished. But I caught my aunt alone at five o'clock in the morning, for the noise of fire-crackers had driven the old creature from her bed at an unwonted hour. I played my cards with all the skill of which I was master. She not only gave me the money, a thousand dollars, which she had " salted down " in the house for fear all the banks would break, but she promised to keep my secret. She declared that Lilian was too extravagant for a young man like me, and I explained that I wished to furnish the house without her knowledge, so as to save expense. She commended my good motive, and I returned to the city with a thousand dollars in my pocket, to furnish the English basement house.

CHAPTER IV.

A THOUSAND dollars in cash was more than I had ever before possessed at one time. I felt like a rich man, for the shadow of the six hundred dollars which I owed did not offensively obtrude itself upon me. I could hardly conceal my exhilaration from Lilian, but I was so intent upon giving her a grand surprise that I kept the great secret, and preserved a forced calmness. I had made very careful estimates of the cost of living in my new palace — I thought they were very careful — and I was fully satisfied that I should save one-third of my present expenses.

My column of figures, after I had thought of every possible expense that could be incurred in the course of the week, footed up at a trifle over twenty dollars a week, but I was entirely convinced that I should bring the actual below the estimated expense. From the first of July my salary was to be two thousand a year, or about thirty-eight dollars and a half a week. I could therefore let my expenses go up to twenty-five dollars a week without upsetting the argument.

Then I allowed three hundred a year for clothing my wife and myself, and for incidental expenses. In our beautiful home we should not care to ride and go to concerts and theatres much, and both of us were well supplied with clothing. I deemed the sum appropriated as amply sufficient. At this rate I could pay off my debts in a year and a half, and be square with the world. Until this was done, I intended to hold myself to a most rigid economy. I must even contrive some way to let Lilian know that I could not spend money so freely as I had done, but I could promise her that, when my debts were paid, she should have every thing she wanted.

I was perfectly satisfied. My prudential calculations set me all right with myself and with the rest of mankind. The vision of the English basement house, all finished and furnished, with Lilian sitting in state in the little boudoir of a parlor, was my castle in the air for the present. I was very cheerful and light hearted, and went to my daily duties at the bank with an alacrity I had never before felt. I told Lilian I should not be at home to dinner that day. When she wanted to know why, I said something about bank commissioners, and was afraid I should be detained until a late hour. She kissed me as usual when I left her, and even " dear ma " looked so very amiable, that I was afraid she would kiss me too. But she did not, and my heart smote me as I thought of the treason I was meditating against her and the two unmarried daughters.

I ought to say here, in justice to myself, that these two sisters of my wife were a heavy burden upon me, independently of the thirty dollars a week I paid for my board; for if Lilian and I proposed to go to a concert, to the theatre or the opera, it was somehow contrived that one or both of them should join the party. My wife reasoned that a carriage would cost no more for four than for two, and the paltry expense of the tickets was all the additional outlay I incurred, while it was *such* a pleasure for the sisters to go. Then I could just as well purchase three pairs of white kids as one — Mrs. Oliphant would pay me for them. I must do her the justice to say that she always offered to do so, but, as it was " all in the family," I was too magnificent to stoop to such trifles; and I know that she would have considered me mean if I had accepted the paltry dollars. I went to the bank with the thousand dollars in my pocket.   I intended to devote the afternoon to selecting the furniture for my new house.   My friend Buckleton was in the furniture business. He would not only keep my secret, but he would give me a bargain on his wares; and what was better, if I came a little short he would trust me. The thousand dollars' worth of goods in my house was so much real property, the possession of which would add to my credit, and was available as security, if occasion required.

The bank closed, and after I had settled my cash, I decided to take a little lunch at Parker's before I went to Buckleton's store. I was going out of the bank when that confounded Shaytop, the stable man, presented himself before me like the ghost of a faded joy.   He had the impudence to thrust his little bill,

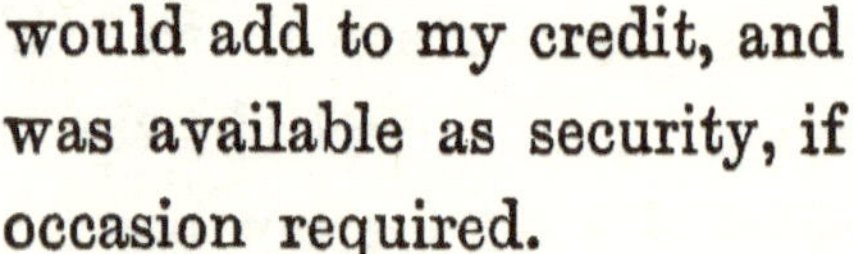

Shaytop's Little Bill.

which amounted to only sixty odd dollars, in my

sunny face. Humph! sixty dollars was nothing to me in my present frame of mind. I didn't "cotton" to any such sum as that, and Mr. Bristlebach, the president of the bank, who was reputed to be worth a million, could not have looked more magnificent than I did, if he had tried.

"Mr. Glasswood, I am getting rather tired of calling on you about my bill," Shaytop began, in the most uncompromising manner.

"Do I owe you anything, Mr. Shaytop?" I inquired, very loftily.

"Do you owe me anything!" exclaimed the fellow, opening his eyes wide enough to catch a vision of the prophetic future. "I reckon you do."

"Is it possible? I declare, I had quite forgotten the circumstance."

"Forgotten it! I'll bet you didn't! I think I have taken pains enough to keep you informed of it."

"Don't be rude, Mr. Shaytop. I don't permit any man to dun me."

"Don't you? Well, by George, you have made an exception in my favor. Haven't I been to see you once a week for the last three months?"

"I don't remember," I replied, vacantly.

"Look here, my gay bird, you can't tom-fool me any longer. I'm going to have my money, or break something," he added, with an energetic gesture.

"Certainly, my dear sir, if I owe you anything, I shall pay it with greater pleasure than you will receive it."

"I'll bet you won't! I want to see Mr. Bristlebach. I don't think he likes to have his clerks run up bills for teams, and not pay for them."

"All right; you can see Mr. Bristlebach, if you wish. He is in the director's room. Shall I introduce you to him?"

"I want to see him if you are not going to pay me."

"Haven't I told you that I should take great pleasure in paying you, if I owe you anything. It had slipped my mind that I owed you a bill, though now it comes to me that there is a small balance due you."

"A small balance! You owe me sixty-two dollars!"

"Well, I call that a small balance. In the bank we deal in big figures. How long have I owed you sixty-two dollars, Mr. Shaytop?"

"About six months."

"Exactly so! Have you added interest?"

" No. I shall be glad enough to get the bill, without saying anything about the interest."

" If I forgot this little matter, it is not right that you should lose anything by my neglect. Add the interest to your bill, and I will pay it."

" That's what you said every time I asked you for the money — all but the interest."

" I'm going up to Parker's for a lunch now. If you will call there in half an hour, I will pay you the bill and the interest," I continued, glancing at the clock in the bank.

" If you mean so, I'll be there."

" Don't insult me, Mr. Shaytop."

" I'll be there, and if you are not there, I'll take the next best step."

He turned on his heel, and left me. It was painfully impressed upon my mind that I must pay that bill, and thus diminish the resources for furnishing the house. But I was something of a philosopher, and I argued that paying this demand would not increase the sum total of my indebtedness; it would only transfer it to the account of the furniture. This thought suggested a new train of ideas. My tailor was bothering me about a little bill I owed him; Uncle Halliard would be asking me again if I did not owe him three hundred dollars; and Tom Flynn would hint that he was short. Why could I not improve my credit by paying off all these debts, and "running my face" for the furniture? It was worthy of consideration as a piece of financial policy.

I went to Parker's, and ordered "a little lunch" which cost me a dollar and a half. Before I had finished it, Shaytop made his appearance. I never saw a fellow look more doubtful than he did. He evidently believed that he had come on a fool's errand. Since I could not well avoid paying the bill, I was to have the pleasure of dissolving this illusion in his mind.

"Sit down, Mr. Shaytop," I began politely, pointing to the chair opposite my own at the table.

"I haven't much time to spare," he replied, glancing at the viands before me, perhaps with the ill-natured reflection that this was the way the money went which ought to be used in paying his bill.

"Won't you have something to eat, Mr. Shaytop; or something to drink, if you please?"

"No, I thank you; I've been to dinner, and I never drink anything."

"Happy to have you eat or drink with me," I added, coolly.

"I'm in a hurry, Mr. Glasswood."

"Are you? Well, I'm sorry for that. We don't live out more than half of our lives on account of always being in a hurry. By the way it seems to me very strange I forgot that little bill of yours. One hundred and sixty-two dollars, I think you said it was?"

"Sixty-two dollars, I said," he answered as if congratulating himself that it was not the sum I named.

He took the bill from his pocket, and laid it on the table before me.

"Good!" said I, glancing at the document. "I'm a hundred dollars in. I was thinking you said it was a hundred and sixty-two."

I intimated to the waiter that he might bring me a Charlotte Russe, and he removed the dishes from the table.

"I don't like to hurry you, Mr. Glasswood, but I ought to be at the stable."

"O, you are in a hurry! I had quite forgotten that you said so.   Well, I will not keep you waiting," I replied drawing my *porte-monnaie* from my pocket.

His eyes glistened, and I think he had a hope by this time. I glanced at the bill again.

"You haven't added the interest," I continued.

5

"Never mind the interest."

" But I am very willing to pay it."

" Well, you add it. You can figure as fast again as I can."

" Sixty-three, eighty-six," I replied. " Receipt the bill, Mr. Shaytop."

He went over to the cashier's desk and performed this pleasing operation. I think the act gave him an additional hope of receiving his money.

"Perhaps you had just as lief take my due bill for six months for this amount, now that we have added the interest?" I suggested.

"No, I'll be hanged if I had!" retorted he, very sharply. " Have you brought me up here, and wasted an hour of my time, to give me your note, which isn't worth the paper you will write it on?"

"You are impudent, Mr. Shaytop."

" Perhaps I am, but —"

"Never mind; if you don't want the note, you can have the money. It don't make much differ-ence to me, though it would be more convenient to pay the bill at another time than now. There isn't the least need of making use of any strong language."

"Pay me, and I won't use any, then."

I opened my *porte-monnaie* and took therefrom the roll of bills I had received from Aunt Rachel. A five hundred dollar bill was on the top, and the balance of the pile was in hundreds and fifties. I ran through the bills with professional dexterity, so that he could see the quality of them.

"I can't make the change, Mr. Shaytop," I replied, with cool indifference.

I glanced at him. I went up in that man's estimation from zero to summer heat. He would have trusted me for a span every day in the week for six months. I took out a hundred dollar bill and tossed it over to him. As I suspected, he could not give me the change. He went to the counter and procured smaller bills for it, and gave me the sum coming to me. He had ceased to be in a hurry.

"If you want any more teams, Mr. Glasswood, I think I can fit you out as well as any other stable in the city," said he, after he had put his wallet back into his pocket.

"I don't," I replied, curtly.

"Don't you ride any now?"

"Yes, just as much as ever; but you see, Mr. Shaytop, I don't like to be bothered with these small accounts, and to deal with men who think so much of little things," I answered, magnificently." You have threatened to speak to Mr. Bristlebach, which you are quite welcome to do; and you intimate that my note is not worth the paper on which it is written."

"I hope you will excuse me for what I said, but I was a little vexed" pleaded he. "I was mistaken in you. The fact of it is, I lost two or three bills—"

"You haven't lost anything by me, and I don't intend you shall," I interposed.

I finished my "little lunch," rose from the table, and having paid my bill, left the house. Shaytop followed me. He wanted my trade, now that he had seen the inside of my pocket-book. But I shook him off as soon as I desired to do so, and hastened to the store of Buckleton. Confidentially I stated my plan to him, and he was willing to be my bosom friend. In the course of the interview I opened my *porte-monnaie*, and contrived that he should see the figures on the bank bills it contained. It was surprising how those figures opened his heart.

When I suggested that I was making a large outlay, he volunteered to trust me to any extent I desired. He was kind enough to go with me to the carpet store, and assist me in the selection of the goods I wanted. I insisted upon paying two hundred dollars on account, which made the carpet people astonishingly good-natured to me; and I was taken aback when they offered to give me credit. Buckleton then went with me to the kitchen furnishing store, and his advice helped me very much as I wandered through the long lists of articles. I made the selection and paid the bill.

When we returned to the furniture store, I warmed toward him, and finally prevailed on him to accept two hundred dollars towards the bill I bought of him. He gave me a receipt. When we footed up the prices of the goods I had selected, I was rather startled to find they amounted to nearly eight hundred dollars.

"I can't afford that!" I protested, "I must go over it again, and take some cheaper articles."

"It don't pay to buy cheap furniture, Glasswood," replied my friend. "You have been very moderate in your selections."

He overcame my scruples by declaring that I need not pay for the goods till it suited my own convenience. I left him and went back to the bank to count my funds. I had only four hundred and seventy dollars left. I could not pay off the six hundred of old debts now; so I left the matter open for further consideration.

The carpet people went to work immediately, and in a week all the rooms were ready for the furniture. Buckleton was so obliging as to go to the house himself and arrange the chairs, tables, bedsteads and other articles. The kitchen furniture was all put in the closets, hung up on the walls, or otherwise disposed of, so that the place looked like an occupied home. I had sheets, pillow-cases, towels, and other articles made up, and in three weeks the English basement-house looked as cosey as the heart of a bank officer could desire.

But fearful inroads had been made upon my exchequer. The carpet people made up a total bill of three hundred and thirty dollars; and when I hinted that I might possibly find it necessary to avail myself of their offer to give me credit, they had a note to pay and wanted the cash. I was too magnificent to haggle. I settled their bill — and cursed them in my heart. When I had paid everything except the six hundred I owed Buckleton, I had only ninety dollars in my pocket.

I was alarmed. A cold sweat stood on my

forehead as I added up the items and found that I was twelve hundred dollars in debt. The situation worried me for a few days, but I soon became accustomed to it. I consoled myself with the hope that the bank would raise my salary, though I could pay off the debts with my present income in three years. It would all come out right in the end, and it was useless to worry about the matter.

I didn't worry long. The English basement house, all furnished, new and elegant, with a Biddy in the kitchen, was a joy which could not be ignored. If it had cost me nearly fifteen hundred dollars to furnish the house, I had that amount of property on hand, and my debts were really no more than before. The house was ready for my wife, and I proposed to her, one afternoon, when all was ready, to take a walk with me.

CHAPTER V

LILIAN ASTONISHED — SO AM I.

IN spite of the doubts and fears which had disturbed me, I was delighted with the English basement house and already in anticipation I enjoyed the surprise of Lilian, when I should tell her that the beautiful home was her own. I asked her to walk with me, but she was a little fretful that day; somehow she seemed more like "dear ma" than I had ever seen her before.

"I don't want to walk to-day, Paley. I'm tired," she replied, with a languid air.

"I only wish to go a little way," I added.

"Not to-day, Paley."

"I want to show you a house, Lilian."

"A house!" she exclaimed with something like an abused expression on her beautiful face, as though she half suspected the treason towards "dear ma" which I was meditating.

"I saw a little English basement house in Needham street, which I would like to have you look at, just as a curiosity, you know," I continued, with as much indifference as I could assume.

"Why do you wish me to see it, Paley?" she asked, exhibiting more interest and apparently forgetting that she was tired.

"Well, because I saw it, and liked the looks of it. There can be no harm in seeing it."

"I don't know, Paley," she answered, doubtfully; but whatever suspicions she cherished, she could have no idea of the truth, "We will go some other day."

"But we may not have the opportunity another day. I happen to know that the house is open to-day."

"What do you mean, Paley? You look just as though you were planning something."

"So I am. I am planning a little walk that will not take half an hour of your time."

"Something worse than that," she added, shaking her head.

"I was thinking that, some time or other, we might possibly go to housekeeping."

"Well, I suppose we shall, some time or other," she answered, languidly. "But I hope you are not thinking of doing it yet awhile. I can't bear the thought of leaving dear ma; we are so pleasantly situated here."

To use a vulgar expression, " I did not see it."
I was not wicked enough to attempt to prejudice
my darling against " dear ma," and I felt obliged
to manage the matter with care. But, as the
shock could not long be deferred, I might as well
make some approaches.

" Of course we are situated pleasantly enough
here; but you know, Lilian, that you said we
must go to housekeeping."

"Certainly, we must go to housekeeping in time,
but not yet."

" But you know that your mother was kind
enough to take us to board only till we could
complete our arrangements. She is very obliging,
and I am very grateful to her for the favor; but
I don't think it would be right for us to impose
ourselves upon her any longer than is absolutely
necessary."

" O — well — of course not; but it will be very
hard for me to go away from home."

" We need not go far; indeed, not so far but
that you can call upon her every day. My conscience reproaches me when I think of the trouble
we are giving her."

" She does not complain."

" She will not complain, but at the same time

it is not right for us to remain here, under the circumstances, any longer than we are compelled to do so. You know she said she should not think of taking any body else to board; and after she has been so kind to us, we ought to be considerate enough not to trespass upon her goodness."

"I will speak to her about the matter; and if she really does not wish to keep us, why, we'll leave," added Lilian.

"But, my dear, you must not forget that she is your mother, and that she will make any sacrifice for your sake, even to her own great injury. It is a matter of conscience with me; and I do not feel like asking her to make this sacrifice of comfort any longer than necessary. Our coming here was only a temporary arrangement, you know, and whatever she may say, our being here will give her a great deal of trouble and anxiety. Come, Lilian, dearest, put on your bonnet. It will do no harm to look at the house. It is already rented to a young couple who are just going to housekeeping," I continued; but I did not think it necessary to say who the young couple were, and she did not seem to care enough about it to ask me.

"If the house is let, why do you wish me to see it?" she inquired.

"I want to get at your ideas in regard to a house," I replied, ingeniously.

She looked at me, and seemed to have some doubts, but she probably reasoned that the house was already rented, and there could be no treason against "dear ma" in merely looking at it. She put on her bonnet and shawl. When my hand was on the door the ever watchful Mrs. Oliphant appeared, and wished to know whether we should be back to tea.

We should; but this was not enough. Lilian was not very well, and she must not walk too far. We were only going around to Needham street, and should return in half an hour. If Lilian was going to call on the Trescotts, why had she not told her mother, for both owed them a call? We did not intend to call on the Trescotts; we were only going out for a little walk. If we were going to walk, why were we particular in saying that we were going through Needham street? There was some treason in Needham street, and Lilian was forced to say that we desired to see a house which was already leased to a young couple who were going to housekeeping.

"Dear ma" looked uneasy, but she permitted us to depart. I was afraid she would insist upon accompanying us, as I think she would, had she not been satisfied by the assurance that the house was already leased. We walked to Needham street. I was full of hope. Lilian would like the English basement house — she could not help liking it, and what a rapturous moment would it be when I told her that it was all her own! Even the anticipated battle with "dear ma" seemed to be farther removed and of much less consequence than before. We approached the house, and my heart beat high with transports of delight. In a few days, perhaps the very next day, I should see the idol of my soul enthroned within its walls!

With Lilian leaning lovingly on my arm, I halted at No. 21. On the door, to my intense confusion and disgust, glittered a new silver plate whereon was inscribed the name, "P. GLASSWOOD," not in Old English, German text, or any other letter which he who runs may *not* often read, but in plain script! I had told the maker not to put it on the door for a week; but he had misunderstood me, or had taken it upon himself to defeat my plan.

" P. Glasswood ! "-exclaimed dear Lilian, stunned and horrified, so that the shock she had thrilled my whole frame.

" Certainly ; P. Glassford," I interposed, promptly. " You know Pierce — don't you, Lilian ? I think you saw him when we were at Springhaven. He is only a second cousin of mine, but he is a good fellow."

" I didn't know you had a cousin of that name," she replied, much comforted.

As I did not know it myself, I did not blame her for not being aware of the circumstance. I opened the door, and we went in, for I had already provided myself with a night key — that gross metallic sin against a wife. Of course the house and furniture were at their best estate. Every thing was new, nice and elegant. The hall gave the first cheerful impression of the house, and Lilian was delighted with it. The little sitting-room was so cosey and snug that my wife actually cried out with pleasure.

The parlors and the chambers were equally satisfactory, and Lilian thought my cousin would be very happy with his bride in this new house. We proceeded to the kitchen, where the Biddy in charge smiled benignantly upon her new " missus, " though she did not betray the secret she had been instructed to keep. My wife was not so much interested in the kitchen as in the parlor and sitting-room, but she was kind enough to say that every thing was neat and convenient, though I am afraid she was hardly a judge on the latter point. We returned to the sitting-room, and my wife seated herself in the low rocking-chair which had been selected for her use.

"How do you like it on the whole, Lilian?" I asked, dropping into the arm-chair, in which I intended to read the Transcript every evening.

"I think it is real nice," she replied, with a degree of enthusiasm which fully rewarded me for all the pains I had taken, and the anxiety I had suffered.

"I'm glad you like it, Lilian. I like it exceedingly, and I am glad to find our tastes are one and the same."

"I don't mean to say that, if I were going to house-keeping, I wouldn't have some things different," she added.

"But you think you could contrive to exist in a house like this?"

"Why, yes; I like it very much indeed."

"Then it is yours Lilian!" I added, rising from

my arm-chair, as I precipitated the climax upon her.

"What do you mean, Paley?" she asked, bewildered by my words.

"This house and all that it contains are ours, dearest Lilian."

"I thought you said it was your cousin's."

"So I did, Lilian; but that was only a little fiction to aid me in giving you a delightful surprise. This house is yours, my dear, and all that it contains, including myself, and Biddy in the kitchen."

"Is it possible? Do you mean so, Paley?"

"I do; every word, syllable, letter and point, including the crossing of the t's and the dotting of the i's, of what I say is true. The house and all that it contains are ours."

"I don't understand it."

"Well, dearest, it is plain enough. Not only to give you a pleasant surprise, but to save you all trouble and anxiety, I have hired the house and furnished it."

"You have, Paley?"

"I have, dearest Lilian! How happy we shall be in our new home."

"I don't think so!"

Certainly Lilian had been duly and properly astonished. It was my turn now, and I was, if possible, more astonished than she had been. She did not think so! What an unwarrantable conclusion!

"You don't think so, Lilian?" I added, interrogatively.

"No, I don't! If you begin in this way we can never be happy."

"Why not?"

"In the first place, I don't want to go to house-keeping yet."

"But I thought you did. The plan has been from the beginning, since we could not get board at the Revere or in Beacon Street, to go to house-keeping," I replied, with rather more sharpness than I had ever before found it necessary to use to dear Lilian.

She was evidently angry, and her eyes glowed like diamonds in the sunlight. But she never looked so pretty as she did at that moment when her face was rouged with natural roses, and her eyes appeared like a living soul.

"Do you think, Paley, that I want to go to house-keeping in a little, narrow contracted box like this?" she added.

6

"I thought you liked the house, dearest Lilian."

"I like it very well for Mrs. Pierce Glasswood, but not for Mrs. Paley Glasswood."

" I am sorry you don't like it, for it is too late now to recede," I replied, gasping for breath. "I was sure it would please you."

"It don't!"

"What possible fault can you find with it?"

"It don't suit me.   How could you do such a thing, Paley, as to hire a house and furnish it, without saying a word to me?"

By this time I had come to the conclusion that it was very stupid in me to do it.

"I wanted to surprise you."

"Well, you have surprised me," she snapped, with such a sweet expression of contempt that I was almost annihilated.   "Do you think a lady has no will of her own? No taste, no judgment, no fancy? How could you be so ridiculous as to furnish a house without asking my advice? Could you have found a homelier carpet in Boston, if you had looked for one, than this very carpet under our feet?"

"Buckleton said it was the handsomest one in the city, and the neatest pattern."

"Then Buckleton has no taste.   No one can

select a carpet for a woman. What did you put that cold oil-cloth on the entry for? I should think you imported it from the polar regions on purpose to give me a chill every time I see it! The figure in the parlor carpet is large enough for a room a hundred feet square. That great blundering tete-a-tete is fit for a bar-room, but not for a parlor. There is no end to the absurdities in this house."

"Now, really, dearest Lilian, I was sure you would be pleased with every thing," I pleaded.

"You are a stupid, Paley Glasswood."

I agreed with her.

"I am very sorry, Lilian; but I did everything with the hope of pleasing you."

"Now here's a pretty kettle of fish!" exclaimed my indignant bride. "What can we do?"

"I can't alter the house, my dear, but I can change the furniture so as to suit you, though doing so will be very expensive," I continued, meekly, as I endeavored to conciliate her.

We had been married only about four months, and the present occasion looked very much like a quarrel. I had not had the remotest suspicion that she was so spunky. It did occur to me that she was slightly unreasonable, if one so beautiful could be unreasonable.   Her father was as poor as a church mouse. His house, as I have hinted, was meanly furnished, and certainly neither the house nor the furniture was worthy to be compared with the one I had provided for my little wife. She had no reason for putting on airs, and being so fiercely critical about the carpets and the chairs. They were vastly better than she had ever had at home.

" Do you think I will live in this house, Paley Glasswood ? " said she, with her lips compressed and her eyes snapping with indignation.

" Why, I hope so," I replied, more astonished than she had been at any time during the visit to the new house.

" You are mistaken, Paley Glasswood. I am your wife, but not your slave ; I am not to be dragged from my home when and where you please. You ought to have told me what you intended to do in the beginning."

"I know it now ; and I confess that I was wrong," I replied, with due humility, and, I may add, with perfect sincerity. " I hope you will forgive me, this time Lilian, and I will never be guilty of such an offence again."

" I should hope not. But here we are ! What's to be done with this house and furniture ? "

" Why, my dear, won't you go to housekeeping
with me ? "

" Certainly not, in this house," she answered,
with a flourish.

This announcement was very startling to me.
It was appalling to think that I had expended
fifteen hundred in preparing a cage which the
bird refused to occupy. Intensely as I loved,
adored Lilian, I could not help seeing that she
was developing a trait of character which I did
not like. But I was a politic man, and seeing
how useless it was to attempt to argue the matter while she was in her present frame of mind,
I had to keep still. We left the house and
walked home. For the first time since we were
married she declined to take my arm, and I began
to be very miserable. Somehow it seemed to me
that the meeker I was, and the more I deprecated
her wrath, the greater became her objection to
the house.

" What shall I say to dear ma ? " demanded
Lilian, after she had thrown off her things.

" My dear, you need not say a word to her. I
will do all this unpleasant business myself," I
replied. " You can lay all the blame upon me.
I will tell her that we are going to our new house
to-morrow."

"You needn't tell her any such thing, for I am not."

Before we had proceeded any farther with the discussion Mrs. Oliphant entered the room. The battle was imminent.

CHAPTER VI

A FAMILY JAR.

I DID not feel at all at ease when Mrs. Oliphant entered the room. I was entirely willing to be conquered and trodden under the little feet of the fair Lilian, but I was not so ready to be trampled upon by the unromantic feet of "dear ma." I was conscious that my pretty wife was getting the weather-gage of me—that she had already got it, in fact. I was not disposed to complain of this, but I intended, if possible, to out-manœuvre Mrs. Oliphant. I regarded Lilian as "my family," and I wished to have her "set off" from my mother-in-law.

In spite of all the strong talk which my lovely wife had used in regard to the English basement house, I confidently expected that she would take her place in the new home I had provided for her. If she was dissatisfied with it, she would soon love it for my sake, if not for its own. But I was sure she did not rebel on her own account; it was the influence of her mother which had controlled her. I accepted the theory that the queen's majesty could do no wrong. If anything was not right, it was the fault of the ministers.

After I had permitted her to say all she had to say, and to exhaust her vocabulary of invective, she would quietly submit to the new house, move in, be as happy as a queen in a short time, and wonder how she had ever thought the little snuggery was not a palace. I had made a fearful expenditure in preparing the house for her; I had thrust my head into the jaws of the monster Debt, and I must make the best of the situation.

"Ma," said Lilian, as her mother entered the room, "what do you suppose Paley has done?"

The poor child looked at the faded carpet as she spoke, hardly daring to raise her eyes to the maternal visage. I hoped she contrasted the hueless fabric on the floor with those bright colors which gleamed from her own carpet in the Needham street house.

"Why, what has he done?" asked Mrs. Oliphan, with a theatrical start, which was modified by a tiger smile bestowed upon me.

"He has hired a house?" replied Lilian, with a gasping sigh, which was simply intended as convincing evidence that she was not implicated in the nefarious transaction.

" Hired a house!"
exclaimed Mrs. Oli-
phant; and her sigh
was g e n u i n e, and
not i n t e n d e d f o r
effect.

" And furnished it
too!" added Lilian,
with horror, as she
piled up the details
of my hideous wick-
edness.

" A n d furnished
it t o o !" groaned
poor Mrs. Oliphant,
sinking into a chair,

Mrs. Oliphant.

as though she had reached the depth of despair in
the gulf into which my infamous conduct had
plunged her.

" He did not say a word to me about the house
or furniture until this very afternoon!" continued·
my beautiful wife, holding up both her pretty white
hands the better to emphasize her astonishment
and chagrin.

" Of course, if you desire to leave your own
pleasant home, Lilian, it is not for me to say a

word," added the meek mamma, with another sigh, which seemed to measure the depth of the resignation that could submit to such an outrage.

"But I do not desire to leave my pleasant home," protested Lilian. "I never had such a thought. I am sure, I have been so happy here that I never dreamed of another home, as long as you were willing to keep us, mother."

"You have been very kind indeed to us, Mrs. Oliphant," I ventured to remark, though I was not certain that the time had come for me to defend myself. "I feel very grateful to you for the sacrifice you have made to accommodate us; and I am sure I shall never forget it."

"A mother lives for her children alone," sighed Mrs. Oliphant. "Even when they are married she cannot lose her interest in them."

"Certainly not, madam; especially not in so good a daughter as Lilian."

"It is hard enough to have them removed by marriage from the direct influence of a mother, and to feel that she is no longer a mother in the sense she has been."

I thought that Mrs. Oliphant had submitted to the marriage of her daughter with tolerable resignation, and would even permit the other two to go to the sacrifice without rebelling. against the dictates of fate.

"Of course she can never be entirely removed from a mother's influence," I replied, wishing that she could. "You have been very kind and considerate toward us since we were married—to me for Lilian's sake."

"And for your own," she interposed.

"I trust I shall never be ungrateful. I feel called upon to explain my conduct," I continued. "You remember, when we returned from our bridal tour that something was said about boarding. We could not find such accommodations as we desired, and you were so kind as to offer to accommodate us till we could obtain a house, or make other arrangements."

"Yes, I remember," replied Mrs. Oliphant. "I don't take boarders, but I was willing to do what I could for Lilian's comfort and happiness."

"You were, madam; and I was very grateful to you for your consideration, both to Lilian and to me. You intimated that it would not be convenient for you to take us to board, but you were willing to sacrifice your own comfort and your own feelings to oblige us. I was very sorry indeed that the circumstances compelled us to trespass upon your kindness.   You did us a favor for which I shall never cease to be grateful.   But I did not feel willing to compel you to submit to the inconvenience of boarding us any longer than was absolutely necessary.   My gratitude compelled me, when I found a house, to take it, and relieve you at once from all the care and responsibility which your self-sacrificing nature had imposed upon you."

"And without even permitting me to see the house in which I was to live!" exclaimed Lilian, coming to the assistance of her mother, who seemed to be thrown into disorder by my tactics.

"I did not suppose it was possible for any one, even with your refined taste, Lilian, to object to such a beautiful little house. But I was obliged to hire it on the instant, or lose it. Another man would have taken it in less than half an hour. It is so near your mother's that you can come to see her half-a-dozen times a day, if you please."

"But I will never live in that house," protested Lilian, with more energy than I thought the occasion required, though I could not help adoring her while her cheeks glowed and her eyes snapped.

"Don't say that, dear Lilian. You should endeavor to conform to the wishes of your husband," mildly interposed the suffering parent. "Doubtless he has done all for the best, and perhaps you will like the house, after all."

"I know I never shall like it," snapped the divine Lilian; which was as much as to say that she was fully determined not to like it.

"Mrs. Oliphant, would you do me the favor to walk over to the house with me?" I suggested to the affectionate mother.

"No; I would rather not. I never step between man and wife," replied she, with praiseworthy resolution. "I do not wish to see the house. This is an affair between you and Lilian, and it is my duty to be strictly neutral."

"But I hope you appreciate my motives?"

"I can not say that I do," she answered. "I think a man should consult his wife before he hires and furnishes the house in which she is to spend a great deal more time than her husband."

I wish to say to my readers that I heartily endorse Mrs. Oliphant's position. A man ought to consult his wife about the house in which she is to spend more of her time than he. It is eminently proper, right and just that he should do so; but I beg to call the attention of the critic to my unfortunate position. Lilian was an angel (in my estimation); her mother was not an angel. The daughter was a mere doll — I am writing after the lapse of years. She was completely under the control of her mother. What I suspected then, I knew afterwards — that Mrs. Oliphant intended to have us as permanent boarders.

Mr. Oliphant had long been running behindhand under the heavy expenses of his extravagant family. Something must be done to eke out his failing income, or the two unmarried daughters could no longer hold their position in society. They must dress, or be banished by their own vanity from the circle in which they moved — a circle which contained husbands. They could not take strangers as boarders, for the house was not fit to accommodate them; but a son-in-law would submit in silence, while a stranger would rebel. I was the victim.

If I proposed house-keeping, my plan would be condemned, as another boarding-place had been already. Perhaps I persuaded myself into the belief, under the necessities of the occasion, that I was hiring and furnishing the English basement house as a pleasant surprise to Lilian. If I did, it was a comfortable delusion, for it was really only a scheme to escape from the clutches of my mother-in-law, and to avoid the martyrdom of my situation on Tremont street. Perhaps the reader will forgive me after this explanation. If he does not, it is not the worst of my errors, and I would thank God most devoutly if I had no graver sin to answer for.

I told Mrs. Oliphant that I had hired a house which was rather better than I could afford; that I had furnished it at an expense which was beyond my means, in order to please Lilian. I said something more about the "pleasant surprise," and was positive that no bank officer of my degree had so fine an establishment. I repeated all I had said about not imposing upon her self-sacrificing nature. But all I said seemed to fall flat upon her ear. She was not touched by my devotion to her daughter ; on the contrary she was disgusted with me, as I read her sentiments in her face, for she did not utter them.

Lilian felt that she had an able champion in her mother, and she said but little. Still professing entire impartiality, Mrs. Oliphant read me a lecture on the impropriety of my conduct, frequently interpolating the discourse with the statement that it was none of her business though, as I had asked her advice (which I had not), she felt obliged to be candid with me. She and Lilian seemed to understand each other perfectly, and while the latter resolutely refused to occupy the house I had prepared for her reception, the former mildly and often declared that a wife should submit to her husband. Lilian knew what to say so as not to implicate her mother in any improper remarks. I think my wife loved me almost as much as she feared her mother. I am sure that she would have accepted the situation with pleasure, if she had not been under her "dear ma's" influence.

What could I do? I had well-nigh ruined myself in fitting up the house. I was vexed, and as the conversation proceeded I began to grow impatient. Finally I left the house to buy some cigars, I said, but in reality to find an opportunity to think over my situation. I did think it over, and I did not buy any cigars, for I was not allowed to smoke them, even in the kitchen. Lilian would yield at once, if she could escape her mother's influence. As it was, I must fight the battle with both of them.

I walked across the Common, thinking what I

should do. If I submitted this time, I should not only be obliged to bear the privations to which the Oliphants subjected themselves in order to maintain their social position, but I must forever be the willing slave of " dear ma." I could not endure the thought. If the family chose to live on tough beef and salt fish, it was their affair, not mine. I could not stand it, and the result of my deliberations was that I decided not to stand it. I went back to the house, stiffened for any thing that might occur, though it almost broke my heart to think of opposing Lilian.

" Perhaps the person who wanted the house you have hired would be willing to take it now, and purchase the furniture you have put into it ? " suggested Mrs. Oliphant, when the subject was resumed.

Perhaps he would ; but my idea just then was that he would not have the opportunity to do so.

" I think not; the party who wanted it would have furnished it at half the expense I have incurred," I replied.

" Couldn't you let it as a furnished house ? " she added.

" My lease does not permit me to underlet it."

" I think it would be cruel to take Lilian away

from her own pleasant home, when she wishes to remain here so much," continued Mrs. Oliphant, a little more sharply than she had yet spoken. "But, of course, it is none of my business and I do not wish to interfere between you."

After supper, I saw Lilian alone in our room. She was as resolute as a little tiger. She positively refused to go into the English basement house, or to have anything to do with it.

"I think you have insulted my mother," she added.

"Insulted her!" I exclaimed, rather startled by this new charge which had evidently been put into her brain by "dear ma."

"She has made her arrangements to board us, and now you want to go away."

"She hasn't made any arrangements at all. Not an article of furniture has been added to the house."

"She says she has; and I think she knows best," retorted Lilian, sharply.

"You have spoken to me every day for a month about furnishing our room."

"I think we ought to furnish it."

"And pay thirty dollars a week for our board! I don't think so," I replied; and this was almost the first time I had ventured to disagree with her.

"Mother says she boards us cheaper than any body else would," snapped my pretty one. "Now you insult her for her kindness to us."

"I have already explained my position to her. I did not mean to insult her, and I don't think my conduct will bear that construction. But, Lilian, the house in Needham Street is all ready for us. I have even hired a servant girl, who is there now."

"I will not go into it, Paley. If you wish to abuse my mother you can, but I will not. I am sorry you have ceased to love me."

"I have not ceased to love you, Lilian," I replied, putting my arm around her neck and kissing her.

Then I went over the whole argument again, and if I did not convince her that I had not insulted or wronged her mother, it was because her fears set logic at naught.

"You will sell the furniture, and give up the house—won't you, Paley?" said she, in her most fascinating way.

"I would if I could Lilian, but the die is cast. I must go, or I am ruined."

Suddenly, in a fit of passion, she shook my arm from her neck and shrunk from me.

"For the last time, Paley, I say it, I will never go into that house," said she, angrily.

"I am sorry, Lilian," I replied, sadly. "You do not act like the loving wife you have always been."

"I will not be insulted any longer."

"Very well, Lilian; I am going to move into the new house to-morrow."

"What!" exclaimed she, aghast, for she evidently did not believe me capable of such rebellion.

"I shall go to the new house to-morrow, after bank hours. If you will not go with me, I cannot help it; and I must go alone."

"Do you mean to say that you will desert me?" gasped she.

"Lilian, I will not pretend to say that what I have done is right, though I did it to please you. I have provided you a house much better than the home of your parents. I have done everything I could to make it comfortable and pleasant. I am sorry I did this without your knowledge, but it is done, and cannot be undone. If you will live in the house for a year or so, and then are not happy, I will leave it. I can do no more to please you."

"I will not move into it!" said she, more bitterly than ever.

I went out of the house, and walked the streets till eleven o'clock at night in utter misery. I returned home. Lilian told me ever so many things her mother had said, and was firmer than ever. The next morning when I went to the bank, I felt like a hopeless martyr.

"Mr. Bristlebach wishes to see you in the director's room, Mr. Glasswood," said the messenger to me.

The president looked stern when I entered the room, and I realized that some charge was pending against me.

CHAPTER VII

A SHADOW OF SUSPICION.

I HAD not sinned against the bank in thought, word, or deed, and I had no fears of the result of an interview with the president. All my sorrows related to my domestic difficulty, which was hardly banished from my mind for a moment, though I did try to imagine what Mr. Bristlebach could possibly want of me. Whatever pecuniary trouble stared me in the face, I had never even been tempted to appropriate a penny belonging to the bank.

"Mr. Glasswood, I have sent for you," said Mr. Bristlebach, sternly.

"Yes, sir; and I am here," I replied, very respectfully.

"When did you balance your cash last?"

"Yesterday afternoon."

"Did it come out right?" .

"Yes, sir," I replied, with the utmost confidence.

"Close the door, if you please."

I did so, and though Mr. Bristlebach did not often take the trouble to spare any one's feelings, this order looked ominous to me. I would give all my earthly hopes at this moment for the con- sciousness of the rectitude of my character which I possessed at that time. I shut the door, and took my stand again in the august presence of the great man—he was great to me, if he was not to others.

" Mr. Glasswood ! " continued Mr. Bristlebach, sternly.

I bowed meekly, to intimate that I was ready to · hear anything he pleased to say.

" Your cash is not right."

" It was right yesterday, at three o'clock," I answered.

" If it was right at three, · it was not at five. I advise you, Mr. Glasswood, to make no denials to any statement which you know to be true. You are a defaulter, sir ! "

Troubles never come singly. It was not enough that I should quarrel with my angelic wife, but I must cross swords with Mr. Bristlebach, who was far from angelic. I might as well find the deep water off Long · Wharf and drown myself. What would Lilian say if I did ? Would she care ? Or would she be only shocked?   Bad as it was, the affair at the bank did not seem half so desperate as the quarrel with Lilian.   I bowed my head meekly to Mr. Bristlebach's charge.   I was innocent, and it did not make much difference to me what the president said.   Under the shadow as I was of a heavier woe than this, it really did not seem worth while to defend myself.

"I say you are a defaulter, Mr. Glasswood," repeated the president, more severely than before.

"No, sir, I am not," I answered, very mildly.

"Have you the effrontery to deny the charge?"

"Yes, sir, I have."

"You have robbed the bank of twelve hundred dollars, at least; and how much more I don't know."

"No, sir; I have not robbed the bank of twelve hundred dollars; nor of even a single cent."

"I am surprised that you should have the hardihood to deny the charge.   Shall I call on your uncle, who is one of your bondsmen?"

"If you please, I do not object," I replied; and I think I should not have objected to any thing.

"Perhaps you will make the bank good yourself?" sneered Mr. Bristlebach.

"I don't owe the bank a penny, sir."

"Mr. Glasswood — sit down!"

I sat down.

"Listen to me, sir!"

I listened.

"I have worked up the case, and understand it perfectly. I am informed that three or four weeks ago you had in your pocket several hundred dollars — perhaps a thousand dollars or more," continued Mr. Bristlebach, whose looks as well as his words were intended to carry confusion to my soul. "Will you do me the favor to say whether or not this statement is true?"

"Quite true, sir. The sum in my pocket-book was one thousand dollars," I replied, beginning to gather up a little light on the subject.

"A thousand dollars! Very well, sir! I am glad you have not the effrontery to deny it. Bank officers in your situation do not usually carry a thousand dollars about with them."

"I do, when I have it to carry, sir."

"Don't be impudent, Mr. Glasswood. Will you deny that this sum was abstracted from the funds of the bank?"

"Certainly I shall deny it, sir. Did Mr. Shaytop inform you that I had taken it from the bank?"

"Who said anything about Mr. Shaytop?" demanded he, sternly.

"I did, sir. It is not very manly in him to accuse me of stealing simply because I refused to hire any more teams of him. Since I was married I have found it necessary to curtail my expenses."

"Do not attempt to dodge the issue, sir."

"I am ready to look the issue fairly in the face."

"You had this money. You confess it."

"I affirm it. I don't confess it."

"Since you had it, perhaps you will not deem it impertinent in me to ask where you got it?" sneered Mr. Bristlebach, who seemed to be as certain that I had robbed the bank as though he had already proved the charge.

"Under the circumstances, sir, I should not deem it impertinent," I replied coolly; and, under the influence of my domestic trouble, I felt rather reckless.

"Well, sir, where did you get it?"

"I borrowed it."

"Precisely so! Borrowed it of the bank!"

"I beg your pardon, Mr. Bristlebach, but there is a wide gulf between my premise and your conclusion. I did not borrow the money of the bank.

If I had, doubtless the paper I offered would have passed under your eyes."

" Mr. Glasswood, your tone and manner do not please me."

" I hope you will excuse me, sir, if I venture to say that the charge you make against me does not please me."

" Will you tell me of whom you borrowed the money ? "

" With pleasure, sir. Of my Aunt Rachel."

Mr. Bristlebach looked at me ; looked sharply at me. He seemed to be a little staggered at something, though, of course, I did not suppose he believed me. He asked me twenty questions about my aunt, all of which I answered with a greater regard for the truth than I was sometimes in the habit of paying to that sublime virtue.

" Mr. Glasswood, your cash is twelve hundred dollars short," he added.

" I was not aware of the fact," I replied.

" After you went away yesterday, I made a strict examination of your department, and you have heard the result."

I was surprised at the announcement, and of course I could not disprove the assertion.

" I can only say, sir, that I left it right at three o'clock yesterday," I added.

"Do you doubt my statement?"

"Certainly not, sir; but I do not understand it."

"The fact that you had a thousand dollars, or any large sum about you, and that you recklessly exhibited it in the dining-room of a hotel, was quite enough to excite my suspicions."

"If I had stolen the money, I think I should not have been so stupid as to exhibit it. If I know myself, I should not."

"But you did show it."

"I did show it; but it was not stolen."

"I think it was; and when I heard of the circumstances, I spent my afternoon here in making the investigation. Perhaps you can put me in the way of verifying your statement that you borrowed the money of your aunt?"

"I shall be very glad to do so. My aunt lives in Springhaven. She will show you my note."

"Even if she does show me your note, and it is fully proved that you borrowed a thousand dollars of her, that will not explain how your cash happens to be twelve hundred dollars short."

"Perhaps I can explain that myself, if you will allow me to examine my drawer," I replied.

Just then a light flashed through my mind, and

I recalled an incident which had occurred just after the closing of the bank on the preceding day, which my private griefs had driven out of my head. I understood it all then, and I was satisfied that I should utterly confound Mr. Bristlebach, though I was, at the same time, in danger of confounding the cashier. But the clock was striking nine, and it was time to open the bank. There was not time to count the cash again, and I did not care to expose a little irregularity on the part of the cashier, by telling what I knew.

Mr. Bristlebach bit his lips and looked at the clock. Through the glass windows of the directors' room, he saw a man come in with a check in his hand. He was evidently deliberating upon the propriety of permitting me to discharge my duties for the forenoon. We were one hand short, and there was no one to take my place.

"Mr. Glasswood, you will not go out of the bank, even for a moment, until this matter is settled. Go to your place, and as soon as the bank closes, we will count the cash again in your presence."

I went to my station, after taking my drawer from the safe. I was now not quite willing to believe that the president considered me guilty. If he did, he would not trust me with the funds of the bank, though he had forbidden me to leave the building. I proceeded in the discharge of my duties as usual, but I soon discovered that the eyes of my superiors were upon me, and if I had been disposed to indulge in a *coup d' etat*, I was too closely watched to permit it to be a success.

Within half an hour after the opening of the bank, the cashier handed me twelve hundred dollars in payment for a draft, which had been placed in my keeping, and which I had deposited in the safe. Just after the bank closed the day before, he had accommodated a friend from my department, by giving him the cash for this draft on a bank, which, for some reasons best known to its officers, declined to pay it after bank hours. It is not for me to discuss the propriety of this action on the part of my superior. It was irregular, and the cashier was personally responsible for his conduct. The draft had been handed to me, and I included it in my cash in balancing.

I learned that the cashier had not been present when the president counted my cash. The book-keeper and receiving teller had assisted him, and as the draft was not in my drawer, the amount appeared to be a deficit on my part. It was very strange to me that I did not think of this transaction sooner.

Perhaps if my family trouble had not perplexed me, I should have done so. But it came to my mind soon enough to correct the impression in the mind of the president, if I had not chosen to suffer rather than betray the irregularity of my superior.

"That makes it all right," said the cashier, as he slipped the bills into my drawer, rather slyly.

"I'm afraid not, Mr. Heavyside," I replied, in a low tone, for Mr. Bristlebach seemed to be all eyes and ears on this forenoon.

"What do you mean, Glasswood?" he asked.

"What time did you leave the bank yesterday?"

"About three. I went out to ride with my wife."

"Where do you get your teams?"

"Of Shaytop. Why do you ask?"

"My cash was examined yesterday afternoon, after both of us left; and I am charged with a deficit of twelve hundred dollars."

"Whew!" whistled Heavyside, more alarmed than I was.

He stood by my side at the counter while I told him that Shaytop "had put a flea into the ear of the president" on my account.

" The scoundrel! I will never drive another of his teams ! " exclaimed the cashier.

Shaytop was not likely to make much by his snivelling operation, which was too mean for any gentleman to appreciate. There was no ground for a charge against me, and I think the stable-keeper made it out of pure malice.

"I said nothing to Mr. Bristlebach about the draft," I continued; "and he still thinks the cash is twelve hundred dollars short."

" This is bad," said he, biting his lips with vexation.

I paid a check, and the cashier walked away to his desk. I saw that he was much disturbed. He was an honest man, in the ordinary sense of the word, and the worst which could be said of the transaction in which he was implicated was that it was simply irregular. He came to me again soon.

" Although this affair amounts to nothing at all, it will cost me my situation, and perhaps my reputation, if the president knows of it," said he.

" He shall not know of it through me," I replied.

" Thank you, Glasswood," he added, warmly; but the conversation was interrupted so that nothing more was said on the subject.

Mr. Bristlebach was a very particular man, but

I do not complain of him on this account. It was proper and right that he should be very exact, and even very exacting, in his requirements. Though Mr. Heavyside had no intention of defrauding the bank of a single dollar, he was imprudent. I believe he did not realize the nature of the act when he obliged his friend out of the funds of the institution. I was fully satisfied in regard to his integrity, and I was more disposed to suffer myself than to excite a suspicion against him.

I am willing now to acknowledge that my position was wrong. The truth should have been told in the beginning. Mr. Heavyside might have been censured, as doubtless he ought to have been, but I do not think he would have been discharged. If he had been, perhaps the tendency would have been to make bank officers more circumspect, more inflexible in the discharge of their duties. It is not safe to step over the straight line of duty even for a moment, for there is no knowing how far one may wander on the wrong side of it.

If this incident did not injure him, it paved the way for me to take a long stride down the road to ruin. When he consented to be sheltered from the displeasure of the president by the cunning of his subordinate, he placed himself, to some extent,

8

in my power. A superior should never sacrifice his dignity before a subordinate, and should never place himself in the attitude of dependence upon him.

The business of the bank went on as usual. My griefs at home had robbed me of my appetite, and I had taken no breakfast. I was not permitted to go out for a lunch, and when the doors were closed my empty stomach and my sleepless night had produced an effect upon me. I was pale and faint, but I was too proud to say anything, and my looks told against me. I could hardly stand up, and doubtless Mr. Bristlebach thought he saw in my wan features and trembling frame abundant evidences of my guilt. He looked triumphant.

The examination of my department was commenced at once. The checks paid were called off, and the bills counted. To the intense astonishment of the president, and, I am sorry to add, to his intense chagrin also, the balance came out all right. There was not a dollar missing. Two counts gave the same result. Mr. Bristlebach was compelled to give it up. I persisted that my account had been squared the day before, but I suggested that some papers had been laid upon a few odd bills which had probably escaped his notice in counting — if I had been present the mistake could not have occurred.

The president stumbled through something which he intended for an apology; and while he was doing so, I absolutely fainted away from sheer exhaustion. Mr. Bristlebach was not a bad man, and I am sure he regretted his inconsiderate accusation. I told him I was not very well, and that the satisfactory result of the investigation was all I desired. I did not blame him. I thanked him for his fairness, and all that sort of thing. From that moment he had more confidence in me than ever — and Shaytop lost another customer.

A cup of coffee and a beefsteak set me right, and I started for my miserable home. I was thinking of meeting Lilian, when my uncle, Captain Halliard, stopped me in the street.

"By the way, didn't I let you have three hundred dollars some months ago?" said he.

"I think you did," I replied, blandly.

He wanted to talk with me, and led the way into an insurance office.

CHAPTER VIII

COMING TO THE POINT.

I WAS not pleased at the meeting, and ventured to suggest that I had important business at home; but my uncle gently dragged me into the insurance office. It was not pleasant to see him just then, and for several weeks I had avoided him, so far as it was practicable to do so. Captain Halliard was a rich man, and it could not possibly make any difference to him whether or not I paid the money I owed him. But I knew that he was exacting.

"I think you said you did borrow three hundred dollars of me," said my uncle, as he seated himself at the long table and took out his pocket-book, evidently for the purpose of finding the note.

"There is no doubt about it," I replied, with what self-possession I could command.

"Just so; I had forgotten the particulars," he continued, as he took the note from the papers in his pocket-book.

He might as well have told me that I had forgotten it, as that he had; but I am sorry to say that both of us had a bad habit of pretending not to remember what, from the nature of the case, must have been uppermost in the mind. It was a stupid and ridiculous affectation. My creditors were often in my mind, and I am sure his debtors were as faithfully remembered.

" I am not prepared to pay the note just now," I began, with more candor than I generally used.

" But, Paley, it is three or four months since I lent you the money; and you promised to pay it in a few weeks."

His memory was improving wonderfully.

" I have just furnished my house, uncle, and that cost me a good deal of money," I pleaded.

" But you got trusted for that," said he, sharply.

" For only a small portion of it," I answered, wondering how he could know that I owed any thing.

" Paley, how much do you owe ? " he demanded.

" O, only a few hundred dollars ! I don't know precisely how much, but not more than I can pay in a short time."

" I'm glad to hear it," replied he, rather dryly. " In how short a time ? "

"In a few weeks."

"That won't do. When I lend money to any one I expect him to pay me, whether friend or foe, in the family or out of it. I'm afraid you are getting along a little too fast."

"I don't think so."

"Your wife is rather extravagant,~I'm told."

"I don't think so."

"Where have you taken a house."

"In Needham street."

"Humph! What do you pay for it?"

"Six hundred dollars."

"Six hundred dollars!" exclaimed he, leaping to his feet.

"A very moderate rent for the house," I added, not at all pleased at what I considered the impudence of my uncle.

"That is more than I pay, Paley. I'm astonished!"

"I think it is a fair rent."

"I don't think so. What did it cost you to furnish it?" he continued, fixing a severe gaze upon me.

"About eight hundred dollars," I answered, not deeming it prudent to give more than half of the actual cost.

" You are crazy, Paley! You will run yourself out in a couple of years, at this rate. Eight hundred dollars! When I was married I didn't spend a hundred dollars on my house. Paley, I will give you three days to pay this note. If you don't do it in that time, I shall do the next thing."

" What's the next thing?" I asked, indignantly.

" I'll trustee your salary!"

" You needn't trouble yourself about the little sum I owe you; I will pay you," I replied, rising and walking towards the door. "The next time I have occasion to ask a favor, I shall not go to a relation."

Doubtless he regarded this as a very savage threat, though perhaps he did not think its execution involved any great hardship on his own part. I walked out of the insurance office with a degree of dignity and self-possession which would have been creditable in a bank president. My uncle must be paid. There was no doubt of that. I would not be thorned by him for all the money in the world, for he was a very uncomfortable sort of man to a debtor, and very obstinately insisted on collecting his dues.

It was patent to me that some one had been talking to Captain Halliard. Perhaps that mischievous stable-keeper had been in communication with him; and it was possible that my friend Buckleton had mentioned the trivial circumstance that I owed him eight hundred dollars. It was not impossible that Mr. Bristlebach and my uncle had been discussing my affairs. They were intimate acquaintances, and the captain did business at the Forty-ninth.

I must pay Captain Halliard, or there would be a tempest about me at once. Not that he would trustee my salary, or anything of that kind; for this was only a hint that he would mention the matter to the president of our bank. I must pay him, but how to do so, was a matter about which I could not venture an opinion. I had little money, and I had already bled my friends as much as it was prudent to

Tom. Flynn.

bleed them. I must "raise the wind," or go under. I walked up State Street, trying to think who should suffer next for my sins, when I met

Tom Flynn. We never passed each other without stopping to speak, though we stood side by side in the bank during business hours. I saw that he looked embarrassed, and it flashed upon my mind before he opened his mouth that he wanted his money, and that he had made up his mind to ask me for it. I did not regard it as proper for him to do so.

"Tom, I'm glad to see you," I began. "I wanted to meet you."

"That's just my case. I was going down to the bank to find you, after calling upon you at Mr. Oliphant's. I wanted to see you very badly;" and the honest fellow looked more embarrassed than ever.

"Well, that's a coincidence," I replied, deeming it my duty to spare him any unnecessary embarrassment. "I have just had a call for a little money I owe, and it was not convenient for me to pay it. It was awkward, because I have a habit of paying up all these little things at sight, even if I have to borrow the money to do so. I shall be flush in three or four days, but I dislike to make this particular fellow wait. Could you lend me a hundred dollars till Monday?"

"I am very sorry, Paley," replied the poor fellow, the wind all taken out of his sails. "The fact is, I'm short myself."

"O, well, never mind it. I'm sorry I said any thing," I continued.

"There was no harm in saying it to me," laughed he, apparently more troubled at my necessity than his own. "I had a chance to buy some stock at a low figure, if I could raise the money to-day, so that the owner can leave to-night for New York. I am one hundred short of the amount required; but no matter; let it go."

"I'm sorry I haven't the amount about me," I replied, with a troubled look. "Perhaps I can raise it for you."

"O, no! I don't want you to do that. You said you should be flush in a few days."

"Yes; I shall have some money on Monday."

"Well, then, Paley, since you can't, help me out, I can help you out," said the noble fellow, with a generous smile. "I can't buy my stock, and you may as well have the money as to let it remain idle."

"Thank you, Tom," I replied, warmly.

"You said a hundred dollars," he continued, stepping into a doorway and drawing out his wallet.

" I said a hundred dollars, but only because I had not the cheek to mention more. I must raise three hundred to-morrow — but only till Monday you know."

" Three hundred," said he musing. " I think I can help you out."

" Thank you, Tom. Next Monday I will pay you this and the other hundred I owe you. And by the way, I had quite forgotten that you held my note."

" It's of no consequence. I haven't wanted it very badly. But I have a chance to invest what little I possess next week, and if I can get it then it will suit me better than to receive it now."

" You shall have the whole next Monday, without fail," I replied, though I had no more idea where the money was to come from than I had of the source of the Nile.

" That will fit my case exactly."

" We will step into the bank, and I will give you a note."

Every body had left the bank except the messenger, and I wrote the note. I had the three hundred dollars .in my fist. I was intent upon taking the sting out of my uncle's tongue. I meant to overwhelm him by paying my note before

I slept. I parted with Tom in the street, and hastened to the insurance office, where I had left Captain Halliard. I found him tipped back in his chair in the inner room, talking with Mr. Bristlebach. I suspected that my case was the subject of their discussion.

"Is that you, Paley?" called my uncle, as I made a movement to retire.

"Yes, sir; but I won't trouble you now, if you are engaged," I replied.

"Come in; we were talking about you, Mr. Glasswood, said the president. "I was just telling your uncle how well satisfied I am with you."

"Thank you, sir. I am very much obliged to you for your good opinion, and I hope I shall always merit it," I added, with becoming modesty.

"Do you wish to see me, Paley?" asked my uncle.

"Only for a moment, sir; but I will wait till you are at leisure."

Mr. Bristlebach took his hat and left the office, saying he had no particular business with my uncle.

"The president of the Forty-Ninth speaks well of you, Paley," said my uncle, good-naturedly.

"I was glad to hear it, for I had a hint that you were going a little too fast. Bristlebach and I talked the matter over yesterday."

"I'm glad you found it all right. Have you my note in your pocket now?" I continued, rather stiffly.

"Yes, I have it."

I drew my wallet, and took out the three hundred dollars I had just borrowed.

"You needn't trouble yourself about that just now," said he, laughing.

"I don't like to be driven into so close a corner as you put me into a little while ago. Here is the amount of the note, with the interest."

"What I said was spoken under a misapprehension. You needn't pay the note till you get ready."

"I am ready now, uncle."

"Of course, I don't object to taking the money; but I didn't mean to press you."

"Didn't you, indeed? You gave me three days to pay the note, and threatened to trustee my salary if it was not paid in that time. If that was not pressing me, I took it as a gentle hint. If I don't know any better than to borrow money of my relations another time, I ought to be hung for being a fool."

"I am sorry now that I said any thing, Paley. I will take it all back."

"Take principal and interest also, and I shall be satisfied."

It was not in his nature to refuse money under any circumstances. He gave up my note and pocketed the amount. It is quite probable that he wondered where I had obtained the funds so readily, and he even hinted at a desire to be enlightened on the subject. Perhaps he would suspect that I had taken them from the vault of the bank; but if he consulted Mr. Bristlebach on the matter, the messenger could inform him that the vault had not been opened during my last visit. To remove any such disagreeable impression as this from his mind, I said something about having a sum of money due me from a friend which I had kept in reserve for another purpose.

After the excellent character which the president had given me, I think my uncle was satisfied. He apologized for the sharpness of his words and declared that he had more regard for my moral welfare than for any thing else. Perhaps he had, but his ideas of moralty were very indefinite, for he had helped me into my situation by pulling down Tom, though I must do him the justice to say that he helped my friend into his present situation, by declaring that new light entirely convinced him of the innocence of Tom.

I left my uncle with the feeling that I had completely overwhelmed him, and made him blush for his conduct. I was satisfied that I could borrow five hundred dollars of him within a reasonable time, and with a reasonable explanation of the necessity. The affairs of the day had improved rather than injured my reputation. My integrity and honesty stood at the highest point. I had made a friend of the cashier, who had stupidly placed himself in my power when open conduct would have served him better in the end. I owed no more than before, but I had hampered myself with a promise to pay Tom Flynn four hundred dollars the next Monday. I had said Monday, because I had a faint hope that I might go down to Springhaven on Saturday and get the amount out of my aunt, who had at least another thousand dollars salted down in her bureau.

There was time enough to think of this matter before the day of payment; but, if the worst came, Tom could easily be cajoled, and even made to insist upon my retaining the money another week or another month. While all these events were transpiring, the unfortunate relations which I sustained to my beautiful wife were hardly out of my mind for a moment. It was nearly six o'clock when I started for home, and all my thoughts were then of Lilian and the new house.

I was tempted to recede from my hard and trying situation, and I probably should have done so if I had not been endowed with a certain obstinacy, sometimes called firmness. It seemed to me that my wife was not my wife while she remained in the home of " dear ma." Her mother had more influence over her than I had, and I could not be happy till I had redeemed her from this bondage. My mother-in-law was swindling me for the benefit of her unmarried daughters. I could not endure it any longer, and come what would come, I would not. I entered the house the saddest and most miserable man in the whole city.

The hour for final action had come. I had informed Lilian that I should move into the English basement house that day. I had ordered an express wagon to come for my luggage at seven o'clock. We had nothing to move but our trunks, in which, for the want of suitable closets, our clothing was still kept. I had seen Biddy in the morning, and told her to have supper for me at half-past seven. I went up to our room. Lilian was there. I saw that she had been crying, but whether from grief or from anger I could not tell. I put my arm around her neck and kissed her, as I always did, when I came into the house.

" You are late, Paley," said she, in forced tones of calmness.

" I was detained at the bank by the president," I replied. " But the wagon will be here at seven, Lilian."

" The wagon? What wagon? " she asked.

" The wagon to take our trunks to Needham Street, Lilian."

" You do not mean that, Paley? " said she, looking up into my face, while her lips quivered and her chest heaved with emotion.

" Of course I mean it, Lilian."

" Do you mean to say that you intend to drag me to that house, whether I am willing to go or not? "

" Certainly not. I have never hinted at any thing of the kind. I only say that I am going; and going at seven o'clock this evening."

" O, Paley! I did not think you would do such a thing! " sobbed she.

9

"I did not think, Lilian, after I had done all I could to please you; after I had carried out the arrangement we agreed upon when we came to board at your mother's; after I had nearly ruined myself in fitting up the house, that you would refuse to live in it," I pleaded. "I acknowledge that I have done wrong, but I cannot help it now. If you will go to the new house with me, I will promise to give it up in a reasonable time, if you are not happy there."

"I will *not* go, Paley! I have said it, and I mean it," said she, spitefully.

"Very well. I am going at seven o'clock," I replied, sadly enough.

I began to pack my trunk, while she sobbed in her chair.

CHAPTER IX.

A LONELY HOUSE.

"DO you mean to desert me, Paley?" asked Lilian, sobbing bitterly.

"Does it look as though I meant to desert you when I have nearly ruined myself to provide a house that would please you?" I replied, as gently as I could speak, for I was not angry.

"But you say you will go to that house without me?" she added, looking up as if she had a gleam of hope that I did not mean what I said.

"I did say so, Lilian. I am going at seven o'clock, when the express wagon comes."

"Don't you call that deserting me?"

"No, Lilian; it will not be that I desert you, but you desert me."

"But I never will go into that house," said she, sharply, as she dashed away the tears that filled her eyes.

"Very well; then we need say no more about it," I answered, placing the last of my wearing apparel in the trunk, and locking it.

"I did not think you would be so cruel, Paley."

"Cruel, Lilian! Do I ask anything unreasonable?"

"I think you do. You come home, and wish to pack me off at half an hour's notice into a strange house."

"I think I spoke of the matter last night, and told you I intended to go. If the time is too short, you may fix a day yourself to move. Name the time you will go, three days, a week, a month hence, and I will not object."

"I shall name no time. I will not live in that house!"

"Then we may as well settle the matter now as at any other time," I replied, with Spartan firmness.

"You will leave me, Paley?"

"I will."

"O, Paley! Have I lost all influence over you?"

"I do not believe in this sort of influence. I repeat that I have done everything to please you; and before I told you that the house was for you, were you not delighted with it?"

This was a sore subject to her. I knew very well that she liked the house herself. Her mother intended to keep us in our present quarters, for the sake of the income to be derived from us. She could board us for ten dollars a week, and make something even at that, for salt fish and round steak form a cheap diet. I estimated that it cost five hundred dollars a year apiece to clothe the two younger daughters, and the profits on my board more than paid the bills. This was the whole matter in a nutshell. I do not think that Lilian was a party directly to the conspiracy, but she knew that it would upset all her mother's plans if we left. Unfortunately for me, I had given the impression that I was made of money; that I not only had a large salary, but that I was the heir of Aunt Rachel, whose wealth was supposed to equal the capital of the Bank of England.

My wife was too proud to acknowledge that she had any interest in her mother's scheme; it was safer to say that she did not like the house. I knew that her family was reduced to the greatest straits; that Mr. Oliphant's income was utterly insufficient to keep up the style of former years. I knew that Mrs. Oliphant pinched herself in every possible way, that the prospects of her two unmarried daughters might not be injured. But I felt that I had done enough for the family when I relieved them of one mouth to feed, and one form to clothe. It certainly was not fair that I should pay the extravagant expenses of making the world believe that my wife's two sisters were fine ladies.

I was fighting the battle for my own independence, and not less for that of my wife. I know that mothers-in-law are shamefully traduced, but only because such a one as Mrs. Oliphant is taken as a type of the whole class. I regard her as the exception, not the rule. Her plan required that she should hold my wife as a slave within the maternal home. In little things, I found that Lilian consulted the will of her strong-minded mother, rather than my feelings. For example, I once overheard Mrs. Oliphant tell my wife to induce me to go to a certain concert, simply because Miss Bertha desired to go. Lilian did induce me to go, and I went. She came up to the point by regular approaches. Not a word was said about Miss Bertha till I was closing the door behind me, as I went to the bank, when it was —" By the way, Paley, don't you think we had better ask Bertha to go with us?" Of course I thought so, and she went with us. Lilian did not care a straw for the concert; neither did I.

This is only a specimen of the manner in which

I was victimized. I not only dressed the two marriageable sisters, but I was to introduce them into society, by paying their bills at concerts, theatres, parties and balls. But this was not the most objectionable part of the arrangement. I could not endure the thought of having my wife made the cat's paw for the monkey to pull the chestnuts out of the fire. She was not my wife, in the just and proper sense· of the word. She did not think so much of my interests and my happiness as she did of her mother's will and wish. Neither of us was to live for each other, but both of us for the Oliphants' ambitious schemes. So thoroughly was I persuaded in my own mind of the justness of my position, that I was determined to stick to it, even if it resulted in a complete separation.

The door-bell rang, and we heard the sound of it in our room. I looked out the window. An express wagon stood before the door. The crisis had come, but I was as resolute as ever, and I expected to spend the night alone in the house in Needham Street.

"A man at the door wants to see you, Paley," said Mrs. Oliphant, who did not keep a servant.

I went down to the door, and brought the man

up with me. Lilian and her mother stood aghast.
They appeared to be utterly confounded, and
neither of them spoke in the presence of the
stranger.

"That trunk," I said to the expressman.

"Is that all?" asked he.

"That is all," I replied, giving him the number
of the house in Needham Street.

The man picked up the trunk and I followed
him down stairs. I paid him, and he went off
with my baggage. I was not willing to leave
my wife without saying good-by to her, for I had
some hope that she would yet relent. When my
hand was on the door which I intended to close,
Lilian called me from the stairs above. She came
down, followed by Mrs. Oliphant. I hoped that
both of them would understand me by this time.

"What's the matter, Paley?" asked "dear ma,"
trying to look pleasant.

"Nothing is the matter," I replied, not caring
to discuss the question with her.

"Lilian tells me you are going to your new
house."

"Doubtless she told you that before."

"But I did not think you would go off and
leave her."

"Such is my purpose, unless she decides to go with me."

"Of course it is not for me to say any thing about it," she added, in her magnanimous way. "But I must say I think you are a little unreasonable."

"Well, Mrs. Oliphant, I don't care about discussing the subject any more. If Lilian chooses to desert me I can't help myself.

"Desert you! Goodness gracious! I should think it was just the other way, and you are deserting her."

"I think not. If I provide a suitable home for my wife, it seems to me that she ought to occupy it with me," I answered, meekly. "I do not wish to be unreasonable, but I think Lilian will admit that our plan discussed, and agreed to while we were on our bridal tour, was to go to housekeeping. I have provided a pleasant house, near yours, and furnished it in a style much better than I can afford. I have told her that, after occupying the house for six months or a year, if it does not suit her, I will conform to her wishes, whatever they may be. I think my view is a reasonable one, and I intend to adhere to it."

"Is she to go there whether she wants to or not?" demanded Mrs. Oliphant.

" Am I to stay here whether I want to or not ? "
I replied. " In the matter of housekeeping, I consulted her, and we were of the same mind."

" You will not leave me, Paley, will you ? "
pleaded Lilian, satisfied that her mother was making no headway in solving the problem.

" No; but you will leave me, Lilian. I am
going now."

" Don't go, Paley ! "

" Will you name a time when you will go with
me, Lilian ? "

" I cannot go, Paley ! Indeed I cannot."

" Good-by then, Lilian," I replied, kissing her,
while the tears gushed from my eyes.

I rushed from the house, without stopping to
close the door behind me. I wiped away my
tears as I crossed the street at a furious pace. I
walked till I had subdued the emotions which
crowded upon me. It was half an hour before I
dared to present myself before the Biddy I had
engaged, lest she should fathom the secret that
worried me. I rang the bell at my house, and
the servant admitted me. She opened her eyes
wide when she saw me alone.

" Where is the missus ? " asked she.

" She has concluded not to come, to-night," I
replied, hanging up my hat in the hall.

"The pretty crayture! Sure I'm dyin' to have her in the house wid me!" exclaimed Bridget. "Is it sick she is?"

Biddy.

"She don't feel very well this evening," I replied evasively.

"Sure the supper is all ready for the two of ye's. The tay is drawn this half hour, and the crame toast is b r e a k i n' in flitters wid waitin' for ye's."

"Very well; I will have my supper immediately."

The tea and the toast were certainly good enough even for Lilian; but it was the most miserable supper to which I ever sat down. My heart seemed to be almost broken. I lighted the gas in the little sitting-room, and threw myself into the rocking-chair. I looked around the apartment. Everything was neat, tasty and pleasant. Was it possible that Lilian refused to share such a palace with me? No; it was not her fault. With her mother's permission how gladly she would have taken her place by my side. Mrs. Oliphant evidently had not given me credit for any considerable amount of resolution. She was " the better horse " in her own matrimonial relations, and she found it difficult to comprehend any other than a similar arrangement in her daughter's family.

I tried to read the newspaper I had brought home with me, but my thoughts were with Lilian. I turned over the leaves of the books I had laid on the centre-table. I went into the dining-room and smoked. I was almost worn out with fatigue and excitement. I was miserable beyond description. I went to bed at midnight, and I went to sleep, but it was only to dream of Lilian, goading and persecuting me, led on by a demon who was always at her side.

I rose in the morning, and found my breakfast ready at the time I had ordered it. It was such a breakfast as Lilian liked, but she was not there to enjoy it, and I groaned in spirit. I must go to the bank. I was not to see my wife, but I decided to write her a line — it was only a line :

" *Dearest Lilian :*—I shall *hope* to find you at our new home when I come up from the bank.

" PALEY."

I sent Biddy to deliver it, and told her not to wait for an answer.

I went to the bank. Everything was "lovely" there. Even Mr. Bristlebach was ." lovely ; " and that was a most unusual attitude for him. Captain Halliard dropped in to see me. He was " lovely." Tom Flynn was in excellent spirits; but he took occasion to tell me something about his business affairs, so that I could distinctly understand what a sad mishap it would be to him if I should fail to pay him the four hundred dollars I owed him on Monday. I felt that I must pay him, and I decided to visit Springhaven on Saturday, and cajole Aunt Rachel into lending me the amount.

I went through my duties mechanically, but that day I lived on hope. I had ordered my dinner at home at half past three, which was the hour I usually dined. Lilian knew my habits, and I felt almost sure that I should find her in Needham Street. I believed that she loved me, and I could not believe that she would desert me. How my heart beat when I went into the English basement house ! How it sank within me when Biddy failed to tell me that the " missus " was there. I dared not ask her any questions, lest she should discover the anxiety under which I was laboring.

I looked into the sitting-room. It was as empty

as the tomb of all I desired to see. I went into the dining-room. The table was set for two, but one of the plates seemed to mock me. Lilian was not there. She was not in the kitchen. I went up stairs, but the same oppressive vacancy haunted every spot in the house. No Lilian was there, and without her the house was not home. The casket and all its appliances were there, but no jewel flashed upon my waiting, longing eyes.

There was no note in reply to mine. Biddy did not deliver any message to me. It was plain enough that she had not heard from the "missus." I was sure that Lilian loved me, and that if left to herself she would come to me, even if I had been lodged in a prison instead of the palace I had provided for her. I ate my dinner alone and in silence. The dinner was a good one, but it would have been the same thing to me if the roast beef and mashed potato had been chips and shavings, so far as I had any interest in their flavor.

When the meal was finished I left the house, and wandered about the streets till tea-time. I kept walking without going anywhere; I kept thinking without knowing what I was thinking about. After I had been to supper, and Biddy had finished her work, she came into the sitting-room where I was looking at the blank sheets of the newspaper I held in my hand. She begged my pardon for coming. She wanted to know when the "missus" was to be at the house. I evaded an answer. She told me she couldn't stay in a house with no missus in it. She didn't "spake to a sowl all day long," and she couldn't "shtop in a house wid only a man in it. She had a char*rack*ter, and people would be talking if she shtopped in a house wid only a man in it." Of course I was utterly confounded at this complication of the difficulty, but I told her that if the "missus" was not able to come by Monday she might go, and I would pay her wages for an additional week.

"God bless your honor! but is the missus sick?" she asked.

"She is not very well, and does not like to leave her mother yet."

She appeared to be satisfied, and I was permitted to spend another miserable night in the loneliness of my new home. I heard nothing from Lilian. I thought she might, at least, send me a note in reply to mine; but I knew that she acted upon the advice of "dear ma." That strong minded woman evidently intended to bring me to terms.   If possible, I was more resolute than ever.

Before I went to the bank the next morning I decided to write one more note—one which could not fail to bring the unpleasant matter to an issue within twenty-four hours.   It was in the form of an advertisement, as follows : —

" Whereas, my wife, Lilian O. Glasswood, has left my bed and board, without justifiable cause, I hereby give notice that I shall pay no debts of her contracting, after this date.

" *Boston, Aug.* —.   PALEY GLASSWOOD.

" Shall I insert the above in to-morrow's papers ?

P. G."

I sent this epistle to Mr. Oliphant's by Biddy. Though it was directed to Lilian, it was intended for her mother.

CHAPTER X

MY WIFE AND I.

I KNEW very well that this note would produce a tremendous sensation in the Oliphant family, and, as I walked down to the bank, I considered whether so violent a demonstration was justifiable. But I soon came to the conclusion that it was not a mere feint, and that if my wife would not live with me in Needham Street, she could not live with me anywhere else. If she did not choose to share my lot in the pretty residence I had provided for her, I would not pay her board in Tremont Street.

I wanted my wife. I had not married Mrs. Oliphant, and was willing to dispense with the benefit of her advice. Perhaps it was reckless in me to do so, but no man had ever made up his mind on any point more decidedly than I had made up mine on this one. I attended to my duties as usual, but there was a sort of grimness about everything I did which astonished me, if it did not any one else.

At my usual hour I rang the bell of my house with a more intense anxiety than had before agitated me. If the savage measure I had taken did not bring Lilian and her mother to their senses, nothing would, and the breach must be regarded as permanent. I hoped and confidently expected to find my wife in the house, and I braced my nerves for the scene which must ensue. Biddy opened the door, with a sweet smile on her face which augured well for my anticipations.

" There's a bit of a letther on the table for ye's, sir," said she, as I hung up my hat in the hall. " Shtop! and I'll bring it to ye's."

" A bit of a letther!" Was that all? Of course it was from Lilian. She did not intend to surrender without conditions. Biddy handed me the missive. It was in my wife's pretty hand-writing, but I was disappointed, and more than ever disposed to be morose. I opened the envelope.

" Come and see me this afternoon, Paley.

" LILIAN."

That was all. The case did not look hopeful. If I went I must fight the battle with " dear ma." I promptly decided that it would be worse than folly for me to heed this request. It was only an ingenious device of Mrs. Oliphant to carry her point by some new strategy. To go would be to throw myself into the toils of the enemy.

Biddy stood looking at me while I read the " bit of a letther." If she did not suspect the trouble, she was more stupid than I supposed. She was a good girl, though her manners needed some improvement. If the wife was ill, the place of the husband was at her side. My gem of the Green Isle could reason out this proposition without exploding her brain. She must understand that a family tempest was gathering.

" Av coorse the bit of a letther is from the missus," said she. " I hope she is betther."

" Is dinner ready, Biddy ? " I replied, trying to laugh.

" All ready, sir. Sure the missus must be betther, for she brought the letther herself.' '

" She is better, Biddy. There is trouble between us."

" Faix, I knew it from the firsht ! "

" Let me have my dinner now, and we will talk about it another time."

She seemed to be proud to have even so much of my confidence, and she flew around with an alacrity which was as creditable to her locomotive powers as it was to her Irish heart. Even her looks were full of respectful sympathy. I sat down to the table, and taking her place behind my chair, she waited upon me with a zeal which would have shamed the black coats of a fashionable hotel.

"In a word, Biddy, my wife refuses to live in this house with me. That's all the trouble we have," said I, as I began to eat my dinner.

"Bad luck to her for that same!"

It was very undignified for me to say anything to my servant, or to any one, indeed, about a matter of this kind, but I was absolutely hungry for a confidant to whom I could pour out my griefs. If the matter was to go any farther, I intended to send for Tom Flynn, and talk over the situation with him. It seemed as though my brain would burst, if I could not relieve it by exhibiting the cause of my sorrows. If Biddy had not known so much I would not have told her any more. I had informed her in the beginning about the "pleasant surprise" I was preparing for my wife. She had seen Lilian when she called, and it was stupid in me to attempt to conceal anything from her. I explained to her the difficulty as far as I deemed it necessary. Biddy was my strongest friend, then. She would not have left me even to save her "char*rack*ter."

She rehearsed the whole matter, declared that I was an angel, and the house a palace. It was not only unreasonable, but cruel and barbarous, for my wife to refuse to share my lot. Thus spake Biddy, and I endorsed her sentiments. When I had finished my dinner I wrote a brief note to Lilian, declining to see her again, until we could meet in "our own house." Biddy was a zealous messenger. She was instructed to deliver it without any words, and without answering any questions, for I was afraid she would take the matter into her own hands, and complicate the difficulty by attempting to fight my battle for me.

An hour later came the reply to my note. Lilian wrote that she was "quite indisposed," and unable to leave the house that day. She wished to see me very much, and begged me not to deny her this favor. Perhaps she was sick. So was I — sick at heart. It would not be strange if the intense excitement attending this affair had made her ill; it had made me so. But I knew she was not so ill that she could not leave the house. She had delivered her own letter in the forenoon when she knew I was at the bank. Yet, if I did not see her when she was sick, it would make the story tell with damaging effect upon me. I decided to see her at once — to see her as my sick wife, and not to make terms in the quarrel.

In five minutes I rang the bell at the door of Mr. Oliphant's house. It was opened as usual by Mrs. Oliphant. A smile of triumph played upon her face as she stood aside to permit me to pass into the hall.

" I am glad you have concluded to come, Paley," said she.

This remark indicated that she was already in possession of the contents of my last note ; in fact that she, and not Lilian, was fighting the battle.

" Is Lilian sick? " I inquired.

" She is not very well."

" I will go up and see her."

I went up.

" O, Paley ! how can you be so cruel ? " exclaimed she, with much nervous excitement.

" Are you sick Lilian? " I replied, taking her hand, and kissing her as though nothing had happened.

" I *am* sick, Paley."

" I am sorry, Lilian."

" Do you think I am made of iron ? "

" Shall I go for Dr. Ingoldson ? "

"I do not need a doctor so much as I need peace."

"We both need that."

"Are you going to drive me into that hateful house?"

"Certainly not, Lilian."

"Did you write that cruel note which came this morning, Paley? I cannot believe it."

"I did write it, Lilian; but if you are sick we will not talk about that," I replied, tenderly, but firmly.

"But we must talk about it. Do you mean to say that you will print that horrid advertisement?"

"Most certainly I shall, if you persist in your present course. It is not right for me to support a wife who will not live with me. If you are sick, we will defer all action until you are better."

"I am not well, but I wanted to see you about this awful business. Have you ceased to love me, Paley?"

"No, Lilian."

Perhaps Mrs. Oliphant had tried to stay down stairs, and permit her daughter to pour out her griefs to me alone; but if she had tried, she had not succeeded; and at this stage of the interview she entered the room, without the ceremony of knocking.

"I am glad you have come, Paley, for we want to talk over this disagreeable business."

"Lilian's note informed me that she was sick, and I came to see her, but not to talk over any matter. If she is ill—"

"She isn't very ill," interposed Mrs. Oliphant.

I thought not; at least not too ill to discuss the exciting topic.

"I am glad she is not very ill. If she is, I will stay at her side and do all that a husband should do for a sick wife."

"O, we can take care of her! But I wanted to ask you if you really intended to put that advertisement into the newspapers?"

"You will excuse me, but I have nothing to say on that subject beyond what I expressed in my note. If Lilian does not need any assistance from me, I will go. If Lilian is ill, I will defer the insertion of the advertisement until Monday morning."

"O, Paley!" gasped Lilian.

"Are you such a monster!" exclaimed Mrs. Oliphant, her lips compressed and her eyes flashing in such a way as to indicate in what manner poor Oliphant had been conquered.

" I have nothing more to say, madam," I replied, with all the dignity I could command.

I moved towards the door. Mrs. Oliphant was proceeding to rehearse the enormity of my offence, when I clipped the wings of her rhetoric by opening the door.

" Good-by, Lilian, if we are to meet no more," I added. " On Monday it will be too late."

I retreated down the stairs, and fled from the house, though Mrs. Oliphant made a lively pursuit as far as the street door, calling upon me with all her might to return.

I know that my lady readers are branding me as a barbarian, but I beg to remind them again that I was not fighting the battle with my wife, but with her mother. I was striking for my own and for Lilian's independence. If I could not have her as my wife, I would not have her at all. I did not go directly home. I called to see Tom Flynn. He was not in, but I left a message for him to see me in Needham Street as soon as he returned.

I was tolerably calm, considering the amount of actual suffering I endured. Biddy was gar-

rulous, and disposed to say harsh things of the
" missus." I checked her, declaring that Lilian
was an angel herself, and that Mrs. Oliphant was
the fomenter of the strife. Fortunately I was
relieved from her comments by the arrival of Tom
Flynn. The noble fellow looked sad when he
entered, and I think he feared I intended to say
I could not pay him the four hundred dollars on
Monday, as I promised. He had not visited my
house before, and he was lavish in his praise of
the good taste displayed in the furniture. Perhaps it suggested him a doubt in regard to the
safety of his money.

" Where is Lilian ? " he asked. "I have not
seen her for a month."

The question opened the subject nearest to my
heart. I began my story, and related it in the
most minute detail up to the interview which
had just taken place between my wife and myself.
The noble fellow was astonished at the recital,
and his countenance beamed with generous sympathy.

" I am very sorry for all this, Paley. It is an
awkward and uncomfortable predicament," said
he.

" What can I do ? "

" I don't know. I think you are right in your main position, though I am not quite so sure in regard to your method of treatment," he replied, musing. "I should not quite like to advertise my wife."

" I don't like to do it; but as sure as my name is Paley Glasswood, I will do it, if she does not come to this house before Monday morning!" I replied, quite excitedly.

" However, I don't think you will have occasion to do it," he added. " Oliphant has had the reputation of being a hen-pecked husband ever since I first heard of him. His wife is a strong-minded woman, and I suppose he found it cheaper to yield than to fight it out. He was a prosperous man formerly, but they say his spirit was broken by this domestic tyranny. I can't advise you to back out, though I wish you had consulted your wife before you furnished the house."

" That would only have transferred the battle-ground to another location. If I yield, I am lost."

It was fully settled with the advice of my friend, that I should not yield. I explained that if Lilian did not like the house or the furniture after a reasonable trial, I would change either or both. Tom Flynn stayed with me till midnight, and told me a great many things in regard to the Oliphants that I was glad to know. It is enough for me to add that I had not misapprehended the character of "dear ma."

The next day was Saturday. I went to the bank at the usual hour, and stayed there till the close of business. I wanted to go to Springhaven that day to make my assault upon Aunt Rachel's purse-strings. The last train left at six o'clock. I was going home, and if my wife did not appear, I intended to spend Sunday at home with my mother. It was the last day of grace, both for Lilian and the money I was to pay Tom Flynn on Monday.

Biddy admitted me, but she had no tidings of my wife. Lilian had not come to my house, and had sent no message for me. Was it possible that Mrs. Oliphant meant to let the affair take its course—to make a "grass-widow" of her daughter rather than allow her to submit? It looked so, incredible as it seemed. After I had eaten my dinner, I wrote a note to Lilian, informing her that I intended to spend Sunday at my mother's, that I would call at our house in Needham Street on Monday morning, and that, if I did not find her there, I should insert the advertisement in all the newspapers. It was then after four o'clock, and I sent the note by Biddy with the usual instructions.

I went up stairs to take a bath and dress for my visit. It was after five when I came down. Biddy had returned, and was busy with her work. I began to tell her where I was going when the door-bell rang.

" Bedad! the missus has come, and brought her mother with her! " exclaimed she, as she rushed into the dining-room where I was smoking away the half hour I had to spare before going to the train.

" Where are they ? "

" In the parlor."

It was not a very encouraging fact that Mrs. Oliphant had come with her. I went into the sitting-room where were seated my guests, for as such only could I yet regard them.

" I am glad you have come, Lilian," said I, entering the room.

" But I have not come to stay," she interposed, promptly.

" Then I am sorry you have come," I added, as promptly.

" It is terrible, Paley, to think that my husband

is prepared to desert me, and to advertise me in the newspapers," said she.

"It is just as terrible for me to be deserted as for you, Lilian. I hope you will think well of it before it is too late."

"I came over to see about this business, Mr. Glasswood," interposed Mrs. Oliphant, stiffly.

"Nothing need be said, madam. I must add that I decline to discuss the question at all."

"That's a pretty way, sir!" continued she. "You married my daughter, and you promised—"

"I know I did, madam, and she promised, too. If she does not choose to occupy the house I have provided for her, that is the end of the whole matter; and also the end of all argument. I am going to Springhaven now. I have nothing more to say, except to add that when my wife returns to me I will treat her as tenderly as I know how, bury the past, and seek only her happiness."

I moved towards the door. Lilian burst into tears. I saw her glance at her mother, who sat in dignified stiffness on the sofa.

"Good-by, Lilian," I said, glancing tenderly at her.

"No, no, Paley! You shall not go!" gasped

she, springing into my arms. " I will stay here ! "

" Lilian ! " exclaimed her mother, springing to her feet.

She was my wife then.

CHAPTER XI.

OVER THE PRECIPICE.

LILIAN was in my arms again, and all that I had
suffered was compensated for by the bliss of
the moment.   I think she had been thorougly aroused
by the peril of her situation, and it was only at
the last possible moment, as she understood the
case, that she yielded.   Lilian was human, like
the rest of the world, and she was fond of her own
way.   I was willing to let her have her own way,
but when it came to giving her mother the control of my affairs, I was rebellious.

My poor wife sobbed in my arms, and I could
hardly restrain my own tears.   I would not have
repressed them if Mrs. Oliphant had not been
present.   Lilian was conquered, but I was sure
she had only reached a point which she had desired
to attain before.   I am not sure that this same
battle is not fought out by every man and wife,
however gentle and affectionate they may be.
Some husbands are brutes, some wives are head-
strong, but each is always jealous of individual

My Wife concludes to stay. Page 160.

power and influence. I think Lilian was disposed
to adopt the tactics of her mother, and rule her
own household; but now she had suddenly
become a gentle and submissive wife, and had thus
placed herself in a position to be potential in regard to her husband.

Mrs. Oliphant was disgusted. She frowned savagely upon both of us. She realized that her influence was gone forever, if this state of feeling
existed. Her cherished plan fell through and was
a wreck beyond the possibility of redemption. I
do not wonder that she was disgusted, for it was
no trivial thing to be suddenly deprived of the
handsome income she derived from me, which I
should have been very glad to pay her, if I could
have done so, though not under the egregious
cheat of paying her thirty dollars a week for board
which was dear at ten.

" Lilian," said Mrs. Oliphant, sternly, " I did
not think you were so weak and childish."

" Weak and childish, mother? Shall I desert
my husband ? " added my wife, gently.

" It is not for me to say any thing, for I never
interfere between man and wife," continued " dear
ma," in the tone of a martyr. " But I can't help
thinking that your husband is very unreasonable.

It isn't every child that has so good a home as you have, and parents who are willing to slave themselves to death for her! And this is all the thanks they get for it!"

"Why, dear ma, what have I done?" asked Lilian, horrified at the implied charge of ingratitude.

"Nothing, nothing! It is no matter!" replied Mrs. Oliphant, with a vigorous effort to appear like a much-abused person. "I suppose it is a mother's lot to be deserted by her children."

"Deserted, mother!" exclaimed my poor wife.

"I would not say any thing, Lilian," I whispered to her.

"After I had made all my arrangements to board you, suddenly, and without a word of notice you go off and leave me. What have I done to merit this treatment?"

Lilian followed my suggestion, and made no reply.

"Well, I suppose I am not wanted here, and I may as well go," she said, flouncing up, and aiming for the door.

"On the contrary, Mrs. Oliphant, we shall both be very glad to have you come here as often and stay as long as you can," I added.

"Yes, mother, my house shall be your house," said Lilian, warmly and with much feeling.

"It is easier to talk than to do," persisted Mrs. Oliphant, who was determined to be an abused person. "I'll go home alone."

"I will go with you, mother if you desire it." interposed Lilian.

Mrs. Oliphant did desire it. It is quite possible she expected still to conquer our united forces.

"Send the wagon for my trunks, Paley, as soon as you please," whispered Lilian, as she left the house with her mother.

I need not say that I lost no time in complying with these stealthy instructions. I hastened for the job wagon, but it was an hour before I reached Mr. Oliphant's with it, for I could not readily find a team at that hour. The clock struck six, and I lost my train to Springhaven; but I hardly noticed the circumstance, so intent was I upon healing the breach in my domestic affairs.

When I arrived at the house, I found Lilian in tears, and a little inclined to yield again; but the appearance of the expressman seemed to strengthen her again. She permitted the trunks to be carried down, and the man departed with them.

"I cannot go, Paley," said she, as she dropped into a chair.

"Why not, Lilian?"

"Mother is terribly incensed against me."

"She will get over it in a few days. What does your father say?"

"Nothing," said she, looking up at me, as though she thought I asked a curious question.

"The sooner we go, Lilian, the better it will be for all of us," I suggested.

"I will go, Paley, but I am afraid I shall never be happy again," said she, rising.

"Yes, you will, my dear. Your mother will be the same as ever by to-morrow."

We went down stairs, and found Mrs. Oliphant in the parlor.

"Good-by, mother. I shall come to see you every day," said Lilian, trying to be cheerful.

"Good-by, Lilian," replied Mrs. Oliphant, in a tone which indicated the depth of her despair.

Lilian said good-by to her sisters, and hoped both of them would come to the house in Needham Street every day, Sundays not excepted. Then we went home. Blessed word! It meant more to me than ever before. I need hardly add that we talked of nothing during the evening but the exciting topic of the day, though I tried frequently to change the subject.

Biddy was the happiest girl outside of Ireland, for though my wife was very sad, she was still the "missus" in her own house. Lilian confessed to me that she liked the house very much; that she would not have had it any different if she had been consulted, but her mother was so anxious to have us remain at her house that she could not think of such a thing as leaving her. If her mother could only be satisfied with the new arrangement, she should be as happy as any mortal in existence.

I hoped for the best. I did not count upon any continued opposition from Mrs. Oliphant, as it was so obviously for her interest to keep the peace now that the Rubicon had been passed. If I had not been so busily occupied in smoothing the path for Lilian, I should have made myself very miserable over my failure to visit Springhaven. I had four hundred dollars to pay on Monday, with nothing on hand to meet the demand. It was an ugly subject, and I avoided it as much as possible in my meditations, though it would often flash upon me. I could not disappoint Tom Flynn.

I took an early walk on Sunday morning, and invited Tom to drop in upon us to dinner that day, which he did. He was delighted to see Lilian in her new home, and congratulated me privately upon the happy issue of the difficulty. In the afternoon Mr. Oliphant called. We showed him all over the house, and the old gentleman appeared to be in raptures. Then Bertha and Ellen came, and they visited every part of the new mansion, expressing their entire satisfaction with all the arrangements.

After church, Tom called again, for he never staid away from service for any reason, forenoon or afternoon. We sang psalm tunes till nine o'clock in the evening, and truly home was home me to then, as it had never been before. Bertha was a splendid singer, and I noticed that Tom, who was very fond of music, appeared to be more interested in her than I had ever before observed. He went home with her, and I ventured to hope that my example would not be without its influence upon him.

When I went to the bank the next morning, Tom told me, in the most careless manner in the world, that Bertha was a very pretty girl, and a magnificent singer. Of course I agreed with him, but the sight of my friend thrust upon me, more forcibly than any other consideration, the ugly fact that I owed him four hundred dollars, due that day. I had not the courage to ask him for further time. My honor, and more than that, my pride, were involved. What could I do?

I might run down to Springhaven at night. No, I could not leave, for, at church and elsewhere, we had invited all our friends to call upon us, and I expected to see company every evening during the week. I must be at home. The money must be paid. There was no possible way by which I could honorably postpone it.

"What time to-day do you want that little matter of money I owe you, Tom?" I asked of my friend.

"As soon after bank hours as convenient."

"You shall have it at half-past two. I must go up the street for it, and can't leave very well before the bank closes."

"All right; it will do at three," added my obliging friend.

What odds would it make to me whether the time was fixed at two or three? I was just as unable to pay it at one time as the other. A lucky thought occurred to me. I could call upon my uncle, Captain Halliard, who would no doubt be glad to redeem his credit with me by lending me any reasonable sum I wanted. In a week or so I could find time to see Aunt Rachel, and as I was her favorite, she would put me in funds.

The bank closed. I was in a tremor of anxiety. Before balancing my cash, I hastened out to find my uncle. He was in the Insurance Office as usual at this hour. I asked him a great many stupid questions about indifferent matters, without daring to put the main question. He actually appeared to have forgotten that he had insulted and offended me. He was rather patronizing and stiff in his manner, and the result of the interview was that I did not mention the matter nearest to my heart. I was sure he would refuse if I did; and I could not be humiliated for nothing.

I was in despair. My heart was in my throat. My pride revolted at the thought of telling Tom Flynn that I could not pay him. I went back to the bank and balanced my cash. I counted over an immense sum of money. Four hundred dollars would make me happy. Mr. Bristlebach had entire confidence in me. Why could I not borrow four hundred dollars of the bank as conveniently as of Captain Halliard.

I trembled at the bare thought of such a thing. Thus far I had kept myself honest before God and man. But then I did not mean to *steal* this sum. I would even put a memorandum in the drawer, to the effect that I was indebted to the bank for this amount. What harm? Who would be wronged by it? I intended to pay every penny of it back in a few days, as soon as I could visit my aunt. It was a little irregular, but even the cashier had done a similar thing within my knowledge. No one would ever know anything about it, and certainly no one would ever lose anything.

Why should I be tortured for the want of four hundred dollars, when thousands were lying idle in my drawer? Why should I humiliate myself before Tom Flynn, when, without wronging any body, I could pay my debt, make him happy, and be happy myself? I was certain that I could return the four hundred dollars. My aunt would certainly let me have it. My uncle even would lend it to me. I had property enough in my house to pay it three times over.

Why should I linger here at the brink of the precipice over which I had determined to leap? I thought, as hundreds of others have thought, in the same trying situation. I comforted myself, as

they have done, with fallacious reasoning. I persuaded myself that, as I intended to pay back
what I borrowed, and convinced myself that I had
the means to do so, it was not dishonest for me
to take the money. I assured myself it was only
a slight irregularity that I meditated; that, even
in the sight of God, it was only a trivial error of
form. The Good Father judges us more by our
intentions than by our acts.

Perhaps I had prepared myself for this step, as
every young man does who permits himself to run
in debt, who allows himself to be continually subjected to a fearful temptation by the pressure
of obligations needlessly incurred. Certainly my
experience in furnishing my house had prepared
me for this temptation. It came when I least
expected it. It was but a trivial form that I
purposed to break through; not the law of honesty, of moral rectitude.

I took four one hundred dollar bills from my
drawer, and slipped them into my vest-pocket.
Everybody in the bank was minding his own business. No one took any notice of me. I think I
must have been as pale as death when I did the
deed, trivial as I chose to regard it. I wrote the
amount in figures, on a slip of paper, and put it

under the bills in the drawer. I convinced myself that this was a suitable acknowledgement of what I had done, which fully relieved me of every intention of doing anything wrong. It is astonishing how weak and silly we are when we are trying to conceal our own errors from our own eyes. The contents of my drawer were transferred to the vault, and I prepared to go home.

"Tom, I haven't had time to get that money yet, but I will meet you at three o'clock, at the reading-room," I remarked to my friend, as easily as I could.

"O, don't put yourself out, Paley," said the generous fellow. "If it is not convenient, let it go."

"No, but it shall be paid. The money is all ready, only I have not had time to go for it."

"I hope the matter has not given you any trouble, Paley," he added ; and perhaps I had not been entirely successful in concealing the anxiety which disturbed me.

"O no, not a bit ! You see my affairs at home took up my time, and I neglected to attend to the matter on Saturday. Be at the reading-room at three, and I shall have the money for you, without fail."

"I will be there, Paley. But what makes you look so pale?" he inquired.

"I don't know. I haven't been very well, and my difficulty at home has worn upon me. But I'm all right now," I replied, assuming a very cheerful face, as I left the bank.

At the appointed time Tom was at the reading-room, and I gave him the four hundred dollars. The bills passed out of my hands, and it was forever too late to undo what I had done. I had leaped over the precipice beneath which lie dishonor, shame and disgrace. I was sorely troubled. My irregularity vexed me, and I felt as one tormented by a legion of devils.

The fact that Tom had noticed my altered appearance put me upon my guard. I tried to be gay and even jovial. I laughed, cracked jokes, rallied Tom on being in love with Bertha—any thing to banish from my mind the corroding feeling that I was a defaulter. I tore up my note which Tom handed to me. I invited him to come to my house in the evening. I invited him to come every evening. I know that I must have talked strangely. There seemed to be a twenty-four pound cannon shot in the centre of my brain. I wanted something to elevate my spirits. I went into a bar-room, and drank a glass of whiskey — a thing I had never before done, though I had taken a glass of wine occasionally.

The liquor inspired me. I drank a second glass, at another bar-room, and found myself capable of rising above my troubles. I went home. Buckleton was there, waiting to see me.

CHAPTER XII

A KEEPER IN THE HOUSE.

LILIAN opened the door, and kissed me as usual when I came home.

"Why, Paley, you have been drinking," whispered she.

"I had a severe pain, and took a glass of whiskey. I feel better now," I replied.

"There's a gentleman waiting for you in the sitting-room," she added.

"Yes, I saw him. It is Buckleton, an old friend of mine. I may ask him to dine with us."

I think Lilian suspected something was wrong with me, though I am sure she had not the remotest conception of the nature and extent of the mischief which was gathering around us. Probably the smell of my breath startled her, with the added fact that I was a little flighty in my manner, for I believe that nothing can be more justly startling to a woman than the possibility of her husband becoming a drunkard. She knew nothing whatever of my financial affairs. I had never made her my confidant; on the contrary, I had weakly and foolishly assumed to be "full of money," and behaved with a liberality and extravagance far beyond my means.

Buckleton was waiting for me. I owed Buckleton eight hundred dollars, for which he had no security. What did Buckleton want with me? It had been his own proposition to give me, under a liberal interpretation of his own words, unlimited credit as to time, if not amount. Why had he come to my house? I had been at the bank all the forenoon, and that was the proper place to meet a man in relation to business. Of course if I had not owed him eight hundred dollars, I should not have troubled my head about this particular visit of an old acquaintance.

However, I had drank two glasses of whiskey, and the circumstance of his coming did not trouble me much. I still felt light-hearted, and was not disposed to let anything trouble me much or long. I smoothed down my hair, and after drinking a glass of ice-water in the dining-room, which my parched tongue required, I entered the room where Buckleton was waiting for me. He was as cordial as though he had come only as an old friend. But exhilarated as I was, I could not fail to notice a certain constraint on his part, as though his cordiality was in a measure forced.

He was glad to see me. He had business at the South End, and thought he would call in upon me as he was passing. The messenger at the bank told me, the next day, he had been there to find me ten minutes after I left. But his coming at this particular time, he labored to represent, was purely an accident. He was glad to see me so well situated. He hoped I should call on him at the West End with Mrs. Glasswood. He had not had the pleasure of knowing my wife, but he hoped to make her acquaintance. All these things he said with the utmost suavity, and then rose from the sofa to take his leave; but he did not take it, and I knew he did not intend to do so until he had said something about the little matter of eight hundred dollars that I owed him. He had his hat in his hand, and moved toward the door.

"Stay and dine with me, Buckleton," I interposed. "Dinner is all ready, and I should be delighted to have you."

"Thank you! Thank you! I should be glad to do so, but I have to meet a gentleman at the store in half an hour," he replied, consulting his watch.

"Let him wait; you needn't be over half an hour behind time."

"I can't do that, for the fact is he owes me some money, and I am desperately short just now."

Bah! I had given him the opportunity to say that, and it was now an easy step for him to dun me.

"Well, come up next Sunday, won't you? And bring your wife with you. We shall be delighted to see you," I continued, hoping to throw him off the track.

"I will, if possible; but I often find that Mrs. Buckleton has made engagements for me, and, if I remember rightly, her father and mother dine with us next Sunday. Besides, I have been so annoyed with business matters for a week, that I have not felt much like going into company. I expected a remittance of six thousand dollars from Havana, and learned the other day that the party had stopped payment. I don't know what we shall do to meet our own notes. By the way, Glasswood, would it be perfectly convenient for you to pay the amount you owe us in a few days?"

"It would not be perfectly convenient," I replied, squarely.

"I know very well that I proposed to wait for

it, but, you see, this confounded Cuban affair throws us all out of groove ; and we are in hot water up to the eyes. Isn't it possible for you to pay it ? "

" Perhaps it is possible, but it would be deused inconvenient. You know I should not have bought so largely if you had not suggested that I might pay for the goods in my own time."

" We sold you, as you are aware, at the very lowest cash prices," he added.

I was not aware of it, but I did not deem it wise to open any controversy on a subject so insignificant.

" I don't see how I can do a thing for you, Buckleton, at present."

" It would be a very great accommodation if you could. Half would be better than nothing, though we want every dollar we can possibly raise. I will discount five per cent. for cash."

" That's liberal, but it won't help me much."

" Think it over, and see what you can do for me, Glasswood. I am in a tight place."

" I am sorry for it, but I haven't got quite settled yet. I shall be able to pay you in a couple of months."

" I may be in bankruptcy before that time," said

he, with a grim smile. " I will call and see you to-morrow morning at the bank."

He went away. I thought I was inclined to stretch the truth quite enough in making out a case, but I could not equal him. He was in no more danger of failing than our bank was. The Cuban matter was a myth. I was satisfied that he had been examining into the condition of my credit. It was more than probable that he had heard rumors of my little difficulty at the bank, and had not heard of the triumphant conclusion of the affair. Shaytop had been whispering in his ear. Very likely my uncle had hinted that I was living too fast. Certainly some persons had been busy with matters which, in my estimation, did not concern them. I was indignant, and felt that I had been abused. Let me say to young gentlemen that shrewd business men usually know us better than we know ourselves, and see sooner than we which way we are going.

Lilian was waiting for me in the dining-room. Of course she wished to know " what that man wanted; " and I turned off the affair as best I could. I sat down, and for a sick man who found it necessary to take medicine, I ate a very hearty dinner.

"Well, my dear, how do you like the house, and housekeeping?" I said, in order to turn the subject from "that man."

"Very much, indeed, Paley. The only drawback is that mother feels so badly about it."

"O, well! she will get over it in a few days."

"Do you know, Paley, that I have been thinking of something?" she continued, looking up to me with that peculiar archness which indicated that she had a plan to propose.

"Have you, indeed? Well, that is not very remarkable."

"I don't know that it is; but why don't you ask me what I have been thinking about?"

"Well, my dear, what have you been thinking about?"

"I'll tell you, since you ask," laughed she. "We haven't had anything like a house-warming yet."

"We have not. That was a great oversight. We will invite our friends, and have some nuts and raisins."

"Nuts and raisins! And be called mean by everybody!"

"Well, what do you propose?" I inquired, though I was rather appalled at the idea of paying the bills for a large party.

" I don't know ; but if we invite all our friends, we must not be mean about it. Besides, I hope mother will come, and then we shall be able to make it all up."

" I hope she will."

We proceeded to discuss the details of the house-warming. Lilian thought it would be cheaper and more stylish to have Smith take charge of the whole thing. He would provide all the eatables, and place a cream-colored waiter in white cotton gloves in the hall to open the door for the guests. She thought it would be more " *re-church-y*," and, of course, I could not stand up against this tre-mendous argument. As I was busy at the bank, she would call and see Smith herself the next forenoon.

She had just been restored to me, and I could not deny her anything. I think it would have broken her heart to know that I was up to my ears in debt ; that I could not afford to pay Smith for even a moderate thing in his line. I ought to have told her the truth, the whole truth, but I had not the courage to do so. I knew very well that the life we had been living at her mother's was just as distasteful and disagreeable to her as to me. She had consented to it for her mother's sake, and had been a martyr since the day we returned from our bridal tour. I need not say that she was fond of style and show, and she had deprived herself of all these luxuries for the benefit of her family. The chain was broken, and the first thing was a party.

I could not help myself without being a tyrant. Smith's bill at the outside could not be over a hundred dollars, and that would not kill me for once. It occurred to me that I would limit the expenses to one hundred dollars, but I did not see how they could exceed this sum; so I decided to let Lilian manage the whole affair to suit herself. I have no doubt she would have done very well, and that the result would have been satisfactory to me, but unfortunately my wife's ideas were different from mine. By an act of grace on the part of a very wealthy gentleman to whom I had been able to render some service, we were invited to a great birthday party of his daughter, shortly after our marriage. Lilian's pretty face and graceful figure made her a great favorite among the gentlemen, and she made quite a sensation. Of course I was proud of her and Lilian deemed it the most fortunate thing in the world to obtain the *entree* of such company.

It never occurred to me that Lilian would attempt to imitate the style of my wealthy friend, or to invite any of the acquaintances she had made there. She knew that I was a bank-teller, on a salary of two thousand dollars, and of course she could not think of competing with a *millionaire*. I went to the bank the next day, and Lilian went to Smith's. While I was looking at the morning paper, Buckleton appeared. He did not seem to have the same suavity which had distinguished him at my house. On the contrary, he was rather stiff and decided in his manner. I told him it was quite impossible for me to pay the bill at present.

"Glasswood, I must be square about this business. Things were not exactly as I supposed, when I sold you those goods. I must have the money or security for the debt at once."

I was mad. Some one had been talking to him about me, and he had listened to the foe rather than to me.

"You seem to be putting a different face upon the affair. Yesterday you were short; to-day you are afraid of losing the money," I replied, coldly.

"I only want to know what you are going to do."

" You told me to pay for the goods when it was convenient. If you had not said so, I should not have bought them."

" Give me a mortgage on the furniture in your house, and I will wait any reasonable time."

"I won't do it! " I replied, angrily.

" Very well; we needn't talk any more about it."

" You professed to be my friend, and were willing to accommodate me."

" Circumstances alter cases. I have different information now."

" What information have you ? " I demanded.

" I am not at liberty to say. I never betray any man's confidence. You are living beyond your means. I am willing to do anything that's fair, but I must have the money or the security."

" I'll see you after bank hours to-day."

" Perhaps you will," said he, leaving the bank very abruptly.

Who had been talking to this man ? I never knew, but I am forced to acknowledge now, what I did not believe then, that his information was correct. I was vexed and disconcerted, and as the forenoon wore away, and my wrath abated, I concluded to give him the mortgage on my household furniture. This matter was so absorbing that I hardly thought of the four hundred dollars I owed the bank till the memorandum I had put in the drawer attracted my attention. I do not know why I tore it up and threw it into the waste-basket, but I did so.

Mr. Bristlebach was very gentle towards me; so was the cashier; and I was confident that no one suspected my cash was four hundred short. The late inquiry into the condition of my department, instead of securing the bank, had opened the way for my first irregularity. I went on with my duties until about one o'clock, when I was not a little astonished to see Biddy come into the bank. My heart rose into my mouth. I was afraid that something had happened to Lilian, and that she was dead or very sick. But Biddy only handed me a note, instead of making the scene I had anticipated.

The note appeared to have been very hastily written, and was not in Lilian's usually careful style. My name was scrawled hastily on the envelope. It occurred to me that Smith might have disappointed her, but I feared something worse than this. I tore open the note. The letter covered two pages, and it was evidently written under great excitement. I was alarmed, and hardly dared to read it, lest it should inform me that one of her family was dead.

I did read it, and it went on to tell me that, while she was away at Smith's, a deputy sheriff had come to the house and attached all the furniture, and left a man there who called himself a "keeper." She had talked with this man, and he had told her Mr. Buckleton was the person who had caused the goods to be attached. These were the material statements of the letter, to which Lilian added that the matter was "horrid;" that she never felt so strangely before in her life. She wanted to know if I really owed Mr. Buckleton a thousand dollars.

I was almost stunned by this heavy blow. Some observations I dropped in regard to Buckleton were not complimentary to that individual. I could not stop to think then. The first business was to quiet Lilian, and I wrote her a note, saying that Buckleton had taken offence at something I had said; that the affair was a mere trifle, and I would send the man away with a flea in his ear when I went home to dinner. I sent Biddy off with this note.

A keeper in my house! What could I do?

CHAPTER XIII.

THE SECOND STEP.

"I TOLD you so!"

It was not easy for me to tell what to do. Eight hundred dollars and all the expenses of the attachment. The keeper was in my house at that moment and poor Lilian appeared to be frightened out of her wits. It was easy enough for me to flourish and call it a small matter, but I could not put my hand upon the money which was to lift the load from my shoulders.

What a crash there would be if this keeper was not driven from the house that very day! What a text it would afford for "dear ma!" How she would declare that it was a judgment

upon me for my wickedness in turning Lilian from
the maternal bosom! How poor Lilian would suffer under this terrible infliction !

It was galling to me even to think of exposing
myself to the fire of Mrs. Oliphant, and I was
willing to drown myself rather than suffer the
punishment she could inflict with her tongue. It
was horrible to anticipate her " I told you so ! "
It would be the sum total of all miseries to be
pitied and advised by her. I must either run
away and leave Lilian to her fate, or pay this
debt; for I could not think of breasting the storm
which would follow an exposure of my financial
condition.

The cold sweat stood on my brow as I thought
of the situation. But I was naturally hopeful and
sanguine. If I had not been so, I should never
have incurred the burden of debt which now
weighed me down. I began to devise expedients;
and Aunt Rachel was always the foremost of
expedients with me. The venerable spinster had
thirty thousand dollars according to the calculations of Captain Halliard, which was one-third
more than I had ever supposed. It was currently
reported, and currently believed, that I was to be
her heir. It was true that the old lady had never

expressed herself to this effect in so many words, but among our friends and relations this theory was fully accepted.

It could make no difference to her if she advanced one or two thousand dollars before she shuffled off her mortal coil. I had so easily persuaded her to let me have a thousand dollars, that I was confident the second thousand would come without much difficulty. If I could only find time to see her, I was satisfied my powers of persuasion would do the rest. I wanted twelve hundred dollars; but this sum would barely cover my pressing liabilities, and I made up my mind that fifteen hundred would come as easily as twelve hundred, and the difference would enable me to meet the cost of the attachment, Lilian's house-warming, and other little matters which would appear before the next pay-day.

I had entire confidence in my own powers. I could put my hand on my heart, and say that I had always treated Aunt Rachel with kindness and consideration. I had always been a favorite with her, and I was positive that the old lady could not resist my eloquence. In fact, I was as sure of the money as though it had already been in my pocket; and as I considered the subject I became hopeful and happy. But I could not go to Springhaven that night, and in a few hours more that abominable keeper might reveal his presence in my house to the whole neighborhood. Lilian did not understand the matter, and if any of her dear friends called, she might relate to them the wretched story I had written in my note.

The keeper must be sent out of the house as soon as I could get away from the bank. His staying there any longer would certainly ruin me. Whatever else was doubtful, this was plain. Tom Flynn stood near me. He had money, though he had just invested all he had in stocks; but I was sure, if I told him the whole truth, he would help me out of the difficulty even if he had to sell his stocks, and sacrifice his dividends. But it was too humiliating to think of telling him that I had plunged into a sea of debt, and was already struggling for life in the waves.

I did think of calling upon my uncle, but I rejected the suggestion on the instant, for I could not listen to the storm of invectives he would heap upon me; and, besides, he would tell my Aunt Rachel, and thus give her a bad opinion of me. The old lady might disinherit me as a "fast boy."

Buckleton had offered to take a mortgage on my furniture for security. This seemed to be the most practicable solution of the problem which had yet presented itself. But what was the use of mortgaging the property when I could pay the debt as soon as I had seen Aunt Rachel? Besides, if there was a man on the face of the footstool whom I hated with all my mind, heart and soul, that man was Buckleton. He had induced me to purchase more extensively than I intended by holding out to me the most liberal terms of credit. Now, in less than a month, he was putting the twisters upon me. I regarded him as a treacherous and unfeeling man; one without a soul; one who would sell his friend for sixpence. I despised him from the deepest depths of my heart, and the idea of asking a favor of him, or even of having a word to say to him, was utterly repulsive to me. I could not see him; I could only treat him with cold and dignified contempt.

Perhaps it was not becoming in one situated as I was to put on such airs, or to attempt to save my dignity. I could not help it. I was proud — I wish I had been too proud to do a wrong deed. There appeared to be no resource to which I could turn for immediate relief. Of the fifteen hundred dollars for which I had decided to ask my aunt, I was perfectly sure. If the old lady hesitated, I could tell her that ruin stared me in the face, that I should be compelled to run away, and never show my face about Boston again, if I did not obtain this money. I was satisfied this threat would bring the money, if nothing else did. I could assure her it would be all the same with her. I would pay her the highest rate of interest, and return the principal in a short time. If she wished it, I could give her security on my furniture for the amount.

I was sure of the money from her. Why should I be distressed for the want of it during the few days that must elapse before I could see her? There was no reason, in my estimation. I need not inform the reader that by this time I meditated taking another loan from the bank funds in my keeping. I could borrow eleven hundred more, thus making my total indebtedness to the bank fifteen hundred. A few days, or even a week hence, I should receive the loan from Aunt Rachel, and I could slip the whole amount in the drawer. Then I should be square with the bank. Then no one would have the power to distress me.

Two o'clock came, and the bank closed. With

far less compunction than I had experienced on the former occasion, I took eleven hundred dollars from my drawer as I transferred the cash to the safe. I did not go through with the idle formality of depositing a memorandum in my trunk with the money. It was a loan for a few days, which Aunt Rachel would enable me to pay. I will not say that I did not tremble — I did. I did not persuade myself that the act was right, only that I intended no wrong. I called the deed simply an " irregularity." It was not stealing, embezzlement, or any other ugly thing with a savage name. I had the money in my pocket, and I think this fact was the basis of all the arguments I used in persuading myself that I had not done a very wicked act.

As soon as I had balanced my cash I left the bank and hastened home. I need not say that Lilian was in a tempest of excitement, in spite of my consoling note. The horrible keeper sat in the dining-room, reading the morning paper, and apparently unconscious of the misery he had brought to my house. He was polite and gentlemanly, and I was magnanimous enough to treat him with consideration. I inquired into the particulars of the case, and proposed to settle the claim at once.

.13

He had no authority to settle it, and referred me to Messrs. Shiver & Sharp, attorneys, in Court Street, who had procured the writ.

Dinner was nearly ready, and I invited the keeper to dine with me. He was condescending enough to accept, and while we sat at the table I did some large talking, in which I was particularly severe upon Buckleton, and particularly complimentary to Glasswood, the latter of whom was a highly honorable man, who had been grossly wronged by the former. Buckleton had put on the attachment out of spite. Glasswood had always paid his debts fairly and squarely, but would not be imposed upon.

After dinner I rushed down to the office of Messrs. Shiver & Sharp. I was indignant and savage, but I was magnificent. I rolled out the hundred-dollar bills with a perfect looseness. I did not even dispute the costs. I paid all, to the utmost penny demanded. Then I talked about the insult, the stain upon my honor, and dilated upon kindred topics, but I fear I failed to make any strong impression upon the astute Mr. Sharp, who conducted the business. He was polite, but he was cold. He gave me a note to the keeper, which I delivered on my return to Needham

Street, and which caused his immediate departure, after he had carefully examined the well-known signature of the legal firm.

"Such things are unpleasant, Lilian, but I suppose they have happened to almost all men at one time or another," I remarked, as soon as the door had closed upon our unwelcome guest.

"I never was so frightened before in my life," she replied with a deep sigh, indicative of the relief she felt.

"It was a miserable trick! It was too mean for any decent man to be guilty of."

"But did you really owe this Buckleton?"

"I did really owe him about eight hundred dollars, but he told me at the time I bought the furniture to pay him whenever it was convenient. It was not convenient to pay him to-day, and he sued me. You know, my dear, that when one has money comfortably invested, drawing large interest, one does not like to disturb it, at least, just before dividends are payable."

"It's too bad!" exclaimed Lilian, warmly, her pretty face beaming with sympathy; and she actually believed that the indefinite pronoun I had used in my description represented myself.

"Well, Lilian, what have you done about the

party ? " I inquired, rather anxious to change the topic, lest she should desire to know more of my financial affairs.

" I have seen Smith, and made all the arrangements for next Friday evening. As it is to be a house-warming, we must not put it off too long. But, dear me, when I came home, and found this awful man here, I was so alarmed that I was on the point of countermanding the order I had given."

" It's all right now. But you must hurry up your invitations."

" There is time enough for them. We will prepare the list this evening. But, Paley, what shall we do for a piano? It will be very awkward to be without a piano on such an occasion. Besides, people will think we are nobody if we don't have one."

" That's very true, Lilian," I replied, somewhat startled by the proposition. " But I'm afraid we can hardly afford to buy one just yet. Such a one as I want would cost five hundred dollars."

" A cheaper one will do."

" But it is bad economy to buy a cheap one. In the course of six months or a year I shall be able to buy a good one."

" We must have one for this party."

"I will see what can be done before Friday."

" And, Paley, you furnished the house beauti-
fully, but there is just one thing for the parlor
that you forgot," continued Lilian, bestowing upon
me her most winning smile.

" What is that?"

" An *étagère*. It would set off the parlor more
than all the rest of the furniture."

" But it would cost about a hundred dollars."

"I would rather do without many other things
than not have an *étagère*," replied Lilian, beginning to look very sad.

" Will you go down town and look at some of
them?" said I, looking as amiable as though I
had not borrowed fifteen hundred dollars of the
bank.

" Dear me! I can't go this afternoon. I have
everything to do. But your taste is so good,
Paley, that you can buy one just as well without
me."

I left the house for the purpose of obtaining a
piano and an *étagère*. Buckleton had showed me
the latter article, and insisted that my house
would not be furnished without it. I had positively refused to buy it, for two reasons. First,
because I could not afford it; and, second, because

no one could pronounce the name of the thing. I confess that it seemed to be a greater sin to place such a piece of furniture where plain Yankees would be tempted to utter its name, than it was to indulge in criminal extravagance. Lilian's French had been neglected, and she made a bad botch of the word, but I decided to instruct her in the difficult task of pronouncing the word.

I went to a piano-forte house. The book-keeper made his deposits and drew his checks over our counter. I know him. He showed me a five hundred dollar instrument. It suited me — the piano, not the price. A lower-priced one did not meet my views. I proposed an arrangement with the concern, that I would hire the instrument with the intention of purchasing if it suited me. One of the firm was consulted. Perhaps he knew that persons who once indulged in a luxury would not willingly give it up. He consented to let it for three months, with the privilege of purchasing at the end of that time. It was ordered to my house. The piano was provided for at an expense of twenty-five dollars, if not bought, for three months.

The *étagère* was a more difficult matter. I could not hire one, and I did not like to pay a hundred dollars for such a useless piece of furniture; but there was no alternative. Lilian had said she must have one. I had nearly three hundred dollars in my pocket, but with this sum I intended to pay Smith, and get rid of my "floating debt," so that I should owe no one but Aunt Rachel. But Smith's bill could not be over a hundred dollars, at the most extravagant figure, and I thought I could spare enough for the *étagère*.

I went to a store near Buckleton's. While I was looking at the *étagère* my late creditor came into the store. I was just closing the bargain at ninety-five dollars. Buckleton had heard from his lawyer, and was glad to meet me. I was glad to have him see me purchase this piece of furniture. He spoke to me. I did not answer him. He attempted to apologize. I did not look at him. I closed my bargain, and asked for the bill. Buckleton was evidently vexed, and felt as any man does when he has lost a customer. I enjoyed it.

"I will sell you that same article for seventy-five dollars," he whispered in my ear, just before I closed the bargain.

"I would not take it, if you would give it to me," I replied.

"I think I made a mistake to-day."

"The mistake of your lifetime," I retorted. "Don't speak to me again. I despise you."

I stalked out of his reach, paid my bill, and went home. In the evening Lilian and I made out the list of invitations. Of course I could not over-rule Lilian's decisions, and not less than fifty were invited — all our house would hold. It included my rich friend's family, and I began to tremble for the result.

CHAPTER XIV

THE HOUSE—WARMING.

HE next day the piano and the *étagère* came, and were duly disposed of in our pretty parlor. I could not help agreeing with Lilian that both of them were absolutely necessary to the proper appointment of the room. After she had covered the *étagère* with a variety of articles, most of which had to be purchased for the purpose, the effect was pleasing.

The piano filled a waiting space; and really there seemed to be nothing more to wish for in this world. Lilian played a few tunes on the new instrument, and my home seemed to be invested with a new charm. Beyond the party, I looked forward to pleasant hours when our friends should gather in this room on Sunday evening to sing sacred music, for which Tom Flynn had a decided partiality.

On Friday morning I went to the bank as usual. When I returned, Smith had taken possession of the house, and was making his arrangements for the grand occasion in the evening. I am bound to say that he made but little fuss for so great an affair When the evening came, a colored gentleman in white cotton gloves was stationed at the door, and more waiters were disposed of in other parts of the house. People came — every body Lilian had invited, except those she wanted most, viz: my wealthy friend from Beacon Street, with his family. They did not come, and I had not supposed they would.

Mrs. Oliphant came, and certainly this was a triumph. Lilian felt that she had outgeneralled her mother, and conquered a peace. I am afraid it required a desperate struggle on the part of " dear ma " to yield the point, and I could only guess at the consideration which induced her to come down from the " high horse." But she was stiff and magnificent at first. She did not seem to enjoy the affair, and looked upon me as an ogre who had defeated all her cherished plans.

Miss Bertha came, and so did Tom; and early in the evening I was not a little surprised to hear the piano giving out the solemn notes of Peterboro and Hebron, sung by a large portion of the company. The instrument was pronounced excellent. Bertha sang like a nightingale, and I am not sure that the piano did not cement a regard which ultimately transformed the fair pianist into Mrs. Tom Flynn.

Everything went well, and at eleven o'clock Smith's supper was uncovered. When I saw the stores with which the table was loaded, I was afraid that the expense would spoil the face of a hundred dollar bill. A little later, when champagne, Madeira and sherry were produced, I was somewhat troubled. Reading the dates on the bottles, I was absolutely alarmed.

"I did not think you intended to have wine, Lilian," I remarked, rather seriously.

"Not have wine!" exclaimed she, after she had imbibed a glass of champagne. "Why, it would be no party at all without wine. I told Smith to bring the best, and plenty of it."

He had evidently done so, and I groaned in spirit.

"Tom Flynn don't drink wine," I added.

"Let him drink coffee, then. We can suit his taste."

"He thinks it is wicked to furnish wine."

"Well, he can have the full benefit of his opinion," laughed Lilian, whose tongue flew merrily under the stimulus of the wine she had drank.

Mrs. Oliphant took champagne, and warmed up under its influence. She became quite sociable, and even forgiving. I was very glad to see that Miss Bertha, for some reason best known to herself, did not partake of the generous beverage. I am not sure that it was not the prospect of disposing of another of her incumbrances quite as much as the influence of the champagne which melted Mrs. Oliphant. Certainly Miss Bertha's chances were very flattering. Psalmody seemed to have done its perfect work.

Tom looked very serious when the wine began to flow in rivers of profusion. He did not like it, and he seemed to be out of his element. While most of the party were eating and drinking in the hall, dining and sitting-rooms, I heard the voices of Bertha and Tom mingling with the notes

The House Warming. Page 204.

of the piano in a sacred song. They were alone in the parlor, preferring to be away from the noisy revel over the wine cup.

Smith's stores of champagne and Madeira seemed to be inexhaustible, and when the clock struck one, some of the party, not excluding a few of the ladies, were in an exceedingly happy frame of mind. Then a dance was proposed, and Tom and Bertha were driven from the parlor. A gentleman played and called the changes. My good friend was actually scandalized by the orgies of the revellers. He never danced; he did not believe in it. Bertha appeared to sympathize with him, though this was not in accordance with her antecedents.

Wine was brought up to the parlor, and the dance went on, though some of my guests were slightly unsteady in their movements. I was shocked to see how wild Lilian was, and I mentally decided that no wine should ever be brought into my house again, for the occasion was now nothing but a revel. Some of the older of the party proposed to go home, and Tom joined them. Miss Bertha was attended to her house by him. When everybody was worn out, the party broke up, and all went away. Lilian dropped into her bed exhausted, and in a measure stupefied. As the hostess, she had been compelled to imbibe oftener than she desired, and really I was grieved to see her in this condition. After all was still, I went through the rooms to see that the windows were secure and the lights put out. I was shocked when I saw what damage had been done to the furniture. The carpets were stained with wine, ice cream and cake ; the new piano was scratched and discolored, and the cloth greased. Besides the cost of this house-warming, whatever it might be, the damages could not be less than three hundred dollars.

At daylight I went to bed, sick at heart. I doubted whether the hundred and fifty dollars in my pocket would pay the bills, and I was miserable. I was in debt at least twenty-five hundred dollars. Lilian slept heavily after the night's debauch. But I could not sleep. What if the bank should discover what I had done? What would the world say the next day, when the particulars of my party were known? for I was satisfied they could not be concealed.

At seven o'clock I got up, my head aching fearfully, for I had not wholly spared the champagne. I was positively miserable. I intended to visit Springhaven that day, and secure the loan from Aunt Rachel. It was not safe to let the matter stand any longer. I went to the bank, and with a throbbing brow attended to my duties. Tom looked very serious, but he did not say any thing to me. Probably he thought I was going to ruin rapidly, not because I had appropriated the funds of the bank, but because I furnished wine to my guests.

The news of my party had not yet been circulated, and I was spared any allusion to it. When I went home I found Lilian had not risen from her bed. She was quite sick. Biddy had done what she could to restore the house to its wonted order, but it was still in confusion. I could not go to Springhaven that day. By Monday morning Lilian was able to get up, and was herself again. She was even willing to acknowledge that such parties " do not pay." I am sure I enjoyed our little Sunday evening gatherings, when Tom and Bertha sang sacred music, much better.

When I went to the bank on Monday, I found Smith's bill enclosed in an envelope. I was afraid to open it at first, but when I did so my worst fears were more than confirmed. The total was three hundred and fifty dollars, of which two-thirds was for champagne, Madeira and sherry. I was appalled and terrified. It must be promptly paid, or Smith would be dunning me. I was short two hundred dollars.

I read the bill a second time, and I was absolutely in despair. My month's salary, when paid, would not make up the deficiency; and I had all my house bills to provide for, which would take up the whole sum. I was running blindly before the wind to destruction. My extravagance would ruin me in a short time. But it was no use to cry. I was in the scrape, and I must get out of it.

My hopeful tendencies came to my aid. With careful economy I could soon pay my debts. A bright idea flashed through my excited brain. Would it not be just as easy to induce Aunt Rachel to lend me two thousand dollars as fifteen hundred? It was a brilliant thought, in my estimation. Five hundred dollars could make no difference to her, if the interest was punctually paid. It was a plain case. If the old lady did not promptly meet my views, I could frighten her into acquiescence. All right! The two thousand was sure enough.

I did not think I should be able to go to Springhaven before Saturday, and I did not care to receive a dunning visit from Smith. I might as well "be hung for an old sheep as a lamb." I could borrow five hundred more from the bank, with no greater risk than I had already incurred —and I did so! My cash was then two thousand short; but before another week had passed, I should get the money from Aunt Rachel, and make good the deficit.

I called upon Smith, and paid the bill. I did not venture to suggest that it was more than I had expected it would be. With so much money in my pocket I felt rich again, and did not bother my head to consider how I had obtained it. I went home in better spirits than for a week. I talked pleasantly and magnificently to Lilian. I had even forgotten my good resolution to practise a rigid economy, for with three hundred dollars in cash in my pocket, it no longer seemed necessary.

Lilian, too, was in excellent spirits. She was very affectionate, and when I sat down on the sofa after supper, she seated herself beside me, and told me how happy she was in her new home, and how glad she was that I had compelled her to move into it. With my head upon her shoulder and her arm around my neck she told me how kind and indulgent, how tender and affectionate I had always been, and then — added that she had not had a new dress since we were married! Mrs. Gordon Grahame had just come out in a splendid black silk; Lilian had never had a black silk, and she wanted one just like it.

"How much will it cost, Lilian?" I asked, rather startled by this ultra-affectionate turn in the conversation.

"You won't be angry with me, Paley — will you?"

"Of course I won't be angry with you, Lilian," I laughed.

"But I have been very economical with clothes."

"I know you have, my dear; and I haven't a word of fault to find. I only asked how much the black silk would cost."

"I can't tell exactly what it will cost," she answered, biting her finger nails, as though she feared even to express an opinion.

"Will it cost fifty dollars?" I asked, thinking I was placing it high.

"Fifty dollars! Why, what an ignoramus you are, Paley!" tinkled she, in the most silvery of tones. "You don't think I can buy a black silk such as a lady would wear for fifty dollars, do you?"

" Well, I don't know any thing about it," I replied, abashed at my own ignorance. " Will a hundred do it?"

" Hardly. I can't tell precisely what it will cost, but I think Mrs. Gordon Grahame's did not cost less than a hundred and twenty. Don't be angry with me, Paley. Don't look so cold!"

" I am neither angry nor cold, dearest," I answered, pulling out my portmonnaie, and taking therefrom one hundred and fifty dollars, which I handed to her.

It was the half I had left of what I had stolen that day — for, in the light of after days, I may as well call the act by its true name. I could not bear to have her accuse me of being angry, or of being cold, or of grudging her any thing I had, or any thing I could get.

" O, thank you, Paley! How generous you are!" she exclaimed, giving me a rapturous kiss.

She was satisfied, and so was I. We talked and read and played backgammon till ten o'clock.

" Paley, won't you take a glass of wine?" she asked. " We had some left the other night."

" I don't care, Lilian. Did I tell you how much that party cost?"

" No."

I told her.

"I think that was quite reasonable, considering what we had. The champagne was splendid, and the Madeira had been to India three times — so Smith said."

She brought a bottle of sherry. It was old and strong. I was rather startled to see her take two glasses within a few minutes of each other, and I wished there was no wine in the house. We went to bed happy, and no thought of the future disturbed me.

The following Saturday was the last day of the month, and I was detained at the bank so late that I could not go to Springhaven. I did not like to leave while others remained, for I did not know but Mr. Bristlebach might take it into his head to overhaul my cash again. The next Monday I learned that Aunt Rachel was very sick, had been attacked with paralysis. I went down to see her that night. She was almost senseless, and I could not talk with her. But she might die in a few days, and then her money would all be mine — I hoped; for it did not yet appear that she had made a will.

Two or three days later, my uncle, Captain Halliard, came into the bank just as we were closing. He looked particularly grim and savage.

"Paley, your aunt is very sick," said he.

"I know she is, but I hope she will get better," I replied, perhaps stretching the truth no more than many people do under such circumstances.

"I am attending to her affairs, as usual."

I bowed, and wondered what was coming.

"I found among her papers a note for a thousand dollars, signed by you," he added, taking the document from his pocket.

My heart came up into my throat. What was he driving at?

"If you can afford to give parties and fill your guests with champagne, you can afford to pay this note," he continued, sternly.

My plan was set at naught.

CHAPTER XV

MY UNCLE IS SAVAGE.

Captain Halliard.

CAPTAIN Halliard was as grim as an ogre, and evidently intended to make me pay the thousand dollars I owed my Aunt Rachel. Of course he did not care half so much about the money as he did to bring me to a realizing sense of the peril of living too fast. He had worked hard for me, and used his influence in obtaining the situation I then held. He was fond of power and influence, and a failure to consult him in regard to any important movement was a mortal insult.

His views of life and living were different from mine, and I found it necessary to steer clear of him. I do not say that this was not a mistake on my part—it was. If I had followed his prudent counsels, I should have kept out of trouble. I had sinned against my uncle, and was no more worthy to be called a *protégé* of his. I had married, I had taken a house, I had furnished it, I had given a party, without consulting him, and even without inviting him to any of the later festive occasions. I knew that they were not to his taste, and it was almost a cause of offence to ask him to attend a merry-making of any kind.

He had lent me three hundred dollars for my bridal tour, though he did not know what it was for—if he had he would not have loaned it to me. He made me pay him when it was the least convenient for me to do so. Now he crossed my path again in the same disagreeable manner. Aunt Rachel was very sick. Probably Captain Halliard had deemed it his duty to look over her papers while she lay insensible on her bed. Notes or interest might fall due. Perhaps it was proper enough that he should do so, but it was deused unfortunate for me.

It was equally unfortunate that I had written this note " On demand, with interest." I had done so because I did not wish to fix a time when Aunt Rachel would feel compelled to ask me for the money. In avoiding a dun in this direction, I had courted one in an other. As sharp people are apt to do, I had overreached myself.

The captain was in bad humor. I had once been his favorite. If I was so now, I was under a shadow. But the case was a very simple one. I had been acting without his advice, and contrary to his well known opinions, which was perhaps very imprudent in me. He was a man of the world, with no fine feelings to interfere with what he regarded as his duty. Of course I could not think of such a thing as paying him. He looked ugly, and my pride was touched by the attitude in which he placed himself.

"Paley, you are going too fast!" said my uncle. sternly.

"I don't think so, sir."

"I think so!" he added, in a tone which was intended to indicate that he regarded the question as settled, and that it would be useless for me to attempt to argue the matter with him.

"I don't know what you mean by too fast," I replied.

"Champagne suppers!"

"Only one, and probably I shall never have another as long as I live."

"You had a party at your house, and the champagne flowed as free as water. Two or three hundred dollars for wine in one evening, as I am informed by one who knows!"

"Who was he?"

"No matter who he was. Deny it if you dare."

"Well, I dare!"

"Show me the bill, then!" said he, fiercely.

I was vexed and indignant at this rude treatment. I forgot that this man had labored to procure my situation ; that he was my mother's brother ; that he had always taken a deep interest in me. I could not bear to be regarded as a child, and be taken to task as such by any one. My pride revolted.

"I don't understand that you are my guardian," I answered.

"I'm not your guardian! If I were, I would send you a hundred miles from the city, and make you work on a farm. I'm the guardian of this note, though ; and it must be paid, or I'll trustee your salary. When you owe your aunt a thousand dollars, you shall not fool away your money on champagne suppers. Pay the note!"

"The note don't belong to you," I added, doggedly, as I beat about me for the means of escaping from the uncomfortable dilemma.

"Don't belong to me!" growled my uncle. "What do you mean by that?"

"How did the note come into your possession?"

"None of your business how it came into my possession, you puppy! Do you mean to insult me?"

"No, sir; but I think you mean to insult me."

"Insult you!" sneered he. "Why, you young cub, I am your uncle, and old enough to be your grandfather!"

"You are not old enough to insult me."

"You have said enough! Will you pay the note?" demanded he, impatiently.

He talked to me as though he were on the quarter-deck, while I belonged in the forecastle. He was not in the habit of permitting his positions to be disputed by those whom he regarded as his dependents or inferiors.

"Not till you have shown me by what authority you hold the note."

"As the agent of the promisee!" snapped he.

"Did she authorize you to collect it?" I inquired.

He drew his out pocket-book, and trembling

with rage and impatience took a document from it, which he thrust into my face. It was a general power of attorney, authorizing him to transact any and all business for my aunt, and ratifying all his proceedings under it. Of course it was dated before Aunt Rachel's present sickness, but I could not deny his power to act under it.

"Are you satisfied?" said he, in a triumphant tone, and he folded up the paper and restored it to his pocket-book.

"I am," I answered.

"Pay then!"

"When do you want the money?" I asked, in a tone of easy indifference, for I saw that I could make nothing by attempting to bluff the old fellow.

"Now!"

"Of course I don't carry a thousand dollars around with me, in my pocket, and I did not expect to be called upon to pay this note to-day. It is not convenient for me to do so."

"I suppose not," sneered my uncle. "But you seem to have money enough to pay for champagne suppers, and better furniture than I can afford to have in my house."

Buckleton was the villain who had been talking to my uncle! "Better furniture" meant the *etagere.* But I must not quarrel with my uncle. He had the power to throw me out of my situation in the bank. As my mother's brother he would not be likely to do that. I was even willing to believe that he was acting for my good, but certainly he was doing so in a very clumsy and ungainly manner. He evidently wished to get me into a tight place, where he could control me, and thus compel me to forego my habits of extravagance.

"Uncle, the champagne supper was a mistake. I did not know there was to be any wine until I saw it. My wife ordered it without my knowledge. I did not suspect she intended to have it, or I should have spoken in season to prevent it."

"Very well; let that pass," said he, considerably mollified. "You have fifteen hundred dollars' worth of furniture in your house. I will sell you all mine for half that sum."

"Buckleton cheated me into taking twice as much as I wanted."

"Humph! Did he?"

"He did."

"Did you pay cash for all these things?"

"Of course I did; though I did not intend to pay Buckleton for a month or two. But he is a scoundrel, and I was glad to get rid of him, even at the expense of sacrificing some stocks I had."

"Stocks?" said my uncle.

"I haven't been so reckless as you think I have," I replied. "I saved two-thirds of my salary till I was married, and doubled it by speculation every year."

"What did you borrow a thousand dollars of your aunt for?"

"Because I didn't wish to sell a thousand dollars' worth of 'coppers' I had, and still have," I continued, knowing very well what would satisfy my uncle. "Somebody was 'bearing' them then; but they are all right now, and I shall make a pretty thing on them by-and-by."

"That's all very well; but you are living too fast."

I was afraid he would ask me what "coppers" I had been dickering in, but he did not, probably reserving an inquiry into the details of my financial operations till we were on better terms.

"I don't think I am living beyond my means."

"I do think so. You must give up that house in Needham Street, and live within your means," he added, sternly.

I actually began to think that he was in league with Mrs. Oliphant.

"I think I can live as cheaply there as anywhere else."

"You can board for half the money it will cost you."

"I differ from you there, uncle, I replied, mildly. "I paid—"

"You differ from me!" exclaimed he, angrily. "Do you think I don't know what I am talking about. I am older than you, and I have seen more of the world. I know what it costs a man to live."

"I think I know something about it."

"No, you don't!" replied he, as arbitrarily as ever. "You can dispose of your lease, and sell your furniture for all it cost you, for houses are scarce."

"I don't wish to do so; the house and furniture are worth as much to me as to any one."

"Paley, you are a fool!" said he, impatiently.

"I came of your stock, then," I retorted, rashly, for my blood was warm again.

"None of your impudence to me!"

"None of yours to me!"

"I am an older man than you are."

"That gives you no right to call me a fool."

"Will you listen to reason?"

"I will, but not to abuse."

"Do you know Brentbone?"

"No, sir."

"He would have taken the house where you live if you had not. While he went to consult his wife you took it."

"I was told that another man would take the house in half an hour if I did not."

"Brentbone was the man. He was terribly disappointed, for he had set his heart upon having the house. He is an old friend of mine, and still wants it. He is willing to give you a hundred dollars bonus for the house, and pay all the bills for the furniture."

"I am much obliged to him for his liberal offer, but I must decline it," I replied, firmly, for I could not think of leaving the English basement house, when I was just beginning to realize the joys of home.

"Are you mad, Paley?"

"Not just now."

"You can't afford to live there. Your mother-in-law will board you at half the rate it will cost you to live in this house."

Upon my word, it looked more and more as if Captain Halliard was in league with "dear ma."

I hate mysteries, and I may as well explain the facts as I afterwards discovered them. Mr. Brentbone was a man of considerable means, who had just married a second wife. The house in Needham Street pleased him, and, too late, he found that it pleased his wife even more. He was acquainted with Mr. Oliphant and with my uncle. When he ascertained who had taken the house, he went to see Mrs. Oliphant, but this was about the time I moved in, and "dear ma" was too indignant to mention the subject to me, though I remembered that she had suggested the idea of selling out the furniture and giving up the lease.

As we had moved in, Brentbone gave up his purpose, and tried to find a house elsewhere. Failing to suit himself, he again turned his attention to the house in Needham Street, and spoke to my uncle about it. Captain Halliard was probably startled to find I was living in a house which would satisfy a person of Brentbone's means. The matter was left in my uncle's hands for negotiation. He assured the would-be purchaser that there would be no difficulty in completing the arrangement. All this Brentbone told me himself in self-defence, a few weeks later, when I made his acquaintance.

As my uncle had in a measure pledged himself to complete the arrangement, he felt a pride in doing so. He honestly and sincerely believed that I was living beyond my means, and here was an opportunity for me to change my style, and make something by it at the same time. He might have succeeded better if he had not begun by attempting to drive me into compliance.

"I have no idea of boarding with my mother-in-law again, and paying her thirty dollars a week for accommodations I can procure for ten," I replied, to my uncle's proposition.

"Then board somewhere else. I don't care where you board; but it will cost you three thousand dollars a year to live in that house."

"I think not."

"I know it will," responded my uncle, sharply.

"Time will tell."

"Leave a fool to his folly," snarled the captain, out of patience with me.

"I will leave you to yours," I replied.

"Will you pay the note?"

"When?"

"Now."

15

"No, sir; I will not."

"When will you pay it?"

"To-morrow," I replied, willing to gain even a day's' delay.

"Very well; if it isn't paid to-morrow, I'll trustee your salary, and keep doing it till the note is paid!" exclaimed he, darting out the ante-room where we had gone to talk over the matter.

I felt very much like sinking through the floor. Not only was I cut off from obtaining the two thousand dollars from Aunt Rachel, but I was called upon to pay the thousand I already owed her. The means of making my account good with the bank were gone, for Aunt Rachel was too sick even to speak to me. What could I do?

I went into the banking-room, and balanced my cash—two thousand short! No one knew it but myself. Mr. Bristlebach was a careful man. He made frequent forays into all the departments of the institution, and the fact could not long be concealed from him. It was about time for the directors to make an examination of the funds. I should be ruined in a few days, or weeks, at most. I could only study how to defer rather than avoid the catastrophe. I put my cash into the safe, and left the building. My face was like a sheet as I saw it in the glass before I left the bank.ʼ My heart was in my throat. I could not see any thing or any body as I walked along State Street.

"Glasswood, how are you?"

I turned to the speaker. It was Cormorin, paying-teller of the Forty-third. I was well acquainted with him, and he lived near my house. He had been present at our party, and had drank more champagne than any other five persons present.

"How are you, Cormorin?" I replied.

"In a hurry, Glasswood?"

"No, not specially."

"Come into Young's with me and drink a bottle of wine."

That was just what I wanted in my misery—something to enliven my spirits. I went, and found that Cormorin had a mission with me.

CHAPTER XVI.

CORMORIN AND I.

CORMORIN was not a man for whom I had ever entertained any great respect, and I wondered how he contrived to retain his position in the bank, for he was rather dissolute and dissipated in his habits. We went to a private room in the hotel, and he sent for champagne. He talked about indifferent matters for a time, but I was soon satisfied that he had something more than these to bring forward. I was not mistaken.

We finished the first bottle of champagne before the plan of my companion began to be developed. He ordered another; but I ought to add, in justice to myself, that he drank three glasses to my one. His frequent potations, however, seemed to have but little effect upon him, for he was accustomed to drink stronger fluids than champagne.

"Glasswood, what salary do you get now?" asked Cormorin, after we had begun upon the second bottle.

"Two thousand," I replied.

" The same as mine. But can you live upon it ? "

" I think I can, though I have not had much experience since I was married."

" I can't live on mine."

" You drink expensive wines."

" 'Pon my soul, I don't ! " he protested. " I haven't tasted champagne, except at your house-warming, for a year, until this afternoon. I can't afford to drink champagne more than once a year ; and I have to stimulate on cheap whiskey. Well, even on this camphene, I can't make the ends meet. I'm as economical as a London Jew. I don't spend a cent on luxuries. I don't go to the opera above a dozen times a year. I don't own a horse. I don't average hiring one more than once a week. I have been in the same fix these two years."

" What do you mean — that you run in debt ? " I inquired, willing to help him reach the point at which he was evidently aiming.

" Just that ; and nothing less, nothing more. I've tried every way in the world to eke out my income ; and, just now, I'm in a fair way to put about ten thousand dollars into my pocket."

" I congratulate you."

"If I had sold my stock to-day, I should have put five thousand into my exchequer."

"Why didn't you do it, then?"

"Because I would rather have ten thousand dollars than five," he replied, gulping down a full glass of the generous fluid before us.

"When a man can make a good thing by selling, I believe in realizing."

"Isn't it better to wait when a man is sure of making twice as much a week hence?"

"Are you sure?"

"I wish I was as sure of living a week as I am of making this money, if I can hold on for a week."

"If I were reasonably certain, I should hold on; by all means."

"O, I'm dead sure! I wouldn't give the president of our bank sixpence to insure me."

"Of course you will hold on, then," I added.

"That's the trouble," said he, slapping his fist upon the table, and then swallowing another potion.

"What's the trouble?" I inquired, kindly asking the questions he suggested.

"Why, the holding on."

"But if you are sure of the result, you cannot be in doubt in regard to your course."

" Well, I'm in no doubt about that."

" What are you in doubt about? "

He looked at me steadily, and appeared to be uncertain whether to say anything more or not. He was struggling to reach some point, though I could not imagine what it was. I began to suspect that he wanted to borrow some money of me. If he did, he had come to the wrong man. He labored heavily, like a ship in a storm, and I was beginning to be rather impatient at the slowness with which he proceeded.

Cormorin and I.

" Glasswood, give me your hand," said he, after a long pause, as he extended his own to me across the table.

I took his hand, for I could not refuse to do

as much as that for a man who was paying for the champagne.

"We are friends—are we not?" he continued.

"Certainly we are."

"Do you mean so?"

"Of course I do. I don't say one thing and mean another. If you want to say any thing, Cormorin, say it."

"As a friend, I will," said he, with compressed lips, as though he had made up his mind to do a desperate deed. "This is between us, you know?"

"Certainly," I replied.

The champagne I had drank had somewhat muddled my brain; and I was in that reckless frame of mind which is so often induced by stimulating draughts. If I had drank nothing, I should have been cautious how I permitted myself to be dragged into the counsels of such a man as Cormorin. As it was, I was becoming rapidly prepared for any desperate step. I was very curious to know what my companion was driving at.

"I'm in a tight place, then!" said he, filling the glass again.

"A tight place! Why, I thought you were on the high road to wealth!" I replied, rather to help him forward in his statement, than because I

experienced any astonishment at his apparent con-
tradictions.

"Exactly so! Both propositions are equally true, and equally susceptible of demonstration. You are dull, Glasswood. You don't drink enough to sharpen your wits. Don't you see that while I am waiting for a further rise in my stocks I am kept out of my capital?"

" Precisely so; that is not a difficult problem to comprehend," I replied.

" Well, you don't seem to get along as fast as I do."

" I understand you now. Go on."

" That's all."

" Let's go home, then," I added, rising from the table.

" Not yet. Hold on! Don't you understand my position?"

" Very clearly; you are short. So am I. If I could help you, I would do so with the greatest pleasure."

" You can help me. We are both honest fellows, and don't mean to wrong or injure any one."

" That's myself for one," I replied, warmly.

He seemed to be using the very arguments

which I had applied to my own case while borrowing the funds of the bank that employed me. What did he mean by it? Could it be possible that he even suspected me of taking the money of the bank? Had he by any means obtained a hint of my financial operations? He was in another establishment. He could not suspect what none in our bank suspected. I was excited with champagne, and I dismissed the fear as preposterous.

"That's myself for another!" exclaimed he, with more emphasis than the subject matter seemed to require. "My coppers have doubled on my hands."

"What are your coppers?" I inquired.

"The Ballyhack," he answered promptly. "Do you think I haven't any?"

He pulled from his breast-pocket a bundle of papers, and exhibited certificates of shares for a very large amount of stock. Just at this time there was a fever of speculation in these copper stocks. While some were substantial companies, many were mere fancies, run up to high figures by unscrupulous and dishonest men. In the particular one he mentioned, the upward progress of the stock had been tremendous. Men had made five or ten thousand dollars in them as easily as they could turn their hands. It was patent to me that the Ballyhack had doubled in a week, and was gaining rapidly every day.

Cormorin had " gone in for a big thing," for he exhibited two hundred shares, for which he had paid twenty-five, and which was now quoted at fifty. Shrewd men were buying it at this rate, confident that the stock would touch a hundred in a week or two. Cormorin's statements, therefore, were reasonable, and I began to be deeply interested in the operation. If this reckless and semi-dissipated fellow could make five or ten thousand dollars in a fortnight, why might not I do the same. It flashed upon my mind that I could redeem myself from my own financial difficulties by this exciting process—if I only had the capital to make the investment. My companion had gone deeply into the business, and could advise me in regard to some safe and profitable speculation in coppers. It would be even less troublesome than borrowing money of Aunt Rachel.

" You see it now," continued Cormorin, folding up his papers, and restoring them to his pocket.

" I do; that's a good operation."

" That's so! What's the use for a man to be

contented with a paltry salary of two thousand a year, when he can make five times that sum in a week or two? That's the question," said he, vehemently.

"It is all very well for a fellow that has the capital to go into these operations," I added.

"The capital! Yes; that's so! There's the rub. But you see I didn't have any capital."

He paused to fill the glasses again, though mine was not empty. He was laboring with the next step in his revelation, and, reckless as he was, he appeared to halt on the verge of further developments. I could not see how he purchased his stock, if he had no capital; and I was rather anxious to have the problem solved.

"Nary red," he added, as I did not ask the question which would suggest the revelation he evidently wished to make. "Not a cent—up to my eyes in debt beside—one, two or three thousand dollars. O, well! When a man understands himself, these things are easy enough. By the way, Glasswood, don't you want to try your hand in this business? I know of a new company, which is going to be the cock of the walk on State Street. You can buy it for twenty to-day. It will be twenty-five to-morrow, for it is going like hot cakes. Everybody is after it. I have been tempted to sell my Ballyhack and invest in it."

" What's the company ? "

" The Bustumup—Indian name, you know. It's going up like a rocket, now."

" Perhaps it will come down like one."

" No fear of that. If I had ten thousand dollars to-day, I would put every cent of it into Bustumups. If you want two, three or five hundred shares of it, I will get them for you at the lowest figure. Your name, you know, would help the thing along."

My name ! Of course I was flattered. If I could have raised four or five thousand dollars, I should have been glad to give the company the benefit of my name !

" I should like to go in, but I have no capital," I replied, with the modesty of a man without means.

" Do as I did ! " exclaimed Cormorin, in whom the champagne had now banished every thing like caution.

" How did you do ? "

" I used the bank funds ! " he replied, hitting the table a tremendous rap. " But I don't mean that the bank shall ever lose a single cent by me. I mean to be honest. I mean to pay every cent I borrow. I don't see why money should lie idle in my drawer in the bank, when I can make something out of it, without wronging, cheating or defrauding man, woman or child. Glasswood, give me your hand. I have spoken frankly to you. If you betray me, of course I shall have to take the next steamer for foreign parts, and I'm afraid the bank would then be the loser by the operation." ·

"I will never betray you," I replied, clasping his offered hand.

"Thank you, Glasswood! You are a noble fellow. To-morrow those infernal directors will examine into the condition of our bank. My cash is five thousand short—just the sum I paid for the Ballyhacks. You understand me?"

I had drank so much champagne that I not only understood, but sympathized with him. He had done just what I had, though I was not stupid enough to betray myself to him.

"I understand you, Cormorin," I replied. "Go on and tell me what you are driving at just as though I were your own brother."

"Exactly so; just as though you were my own

brother. I borrowed five thousand dollars from the bank. It will be missed to-morrow. Lend me five one thousand dollar bills, or the same amount in some other form, for two hours to-morrow, and I shall be all right. You shall hold my stock as collateral. It is worth double the amount; and I will do the same thing for you when your cash is counted, if you want to make something on your own account."

"I'll do it," I replied, without a moment of reflection.

"You are a good fellow, Glasswood. Your fortune is made, and so is mine."

I should not have been so prompt in acceding to his request without the aid of the champagne. Though I knew what I was about well enough, I was reckless. I was fascinated with the idea of making five or ten thousand dollars in "coppers," and thus discharging my obligation to the bank.

"We don't always know when our directors intend to make an examination," I suggested.

"I can always tell by the looks of them. No matter; there is time enough after they begin. Our banks are near enough to each other to enable us to make a connection," laughed Cormorin.

We discussed the matter still further, but we were perfectly agreed. We separated with an arrangement to meet in the forenoon of the next day, to carry out the plan we had devised. I did not deem it prudent to go directly home, and I spent an hour on the Common, waiting for the fumes of the wine I had drank to work off. When I went to Needham Street, I found that Lilian was still out, probably purchasing her new black silk dress. She came at last, and we ate a dried-up dinner at five o'clock. She had purchased her dress, and was in the best of spirits.

The next day, when I went to the bank, I quietly transferred six thousand dollars from my drawer to my pocket, with hardly a tithe of the compunction with which I had appropriated my first loan. O, I intended to be honest! The bank was not to lose a penny by me. For five thousand of the money, Cormorin was to give me collateral worth ten thousand in the market. With the other thousand I intended to pay my uncle, and silence his carping for all time.

Cormorin was punctual in his call for his share of the funds. He handed me the certificates and I gave him the money. In the course of the forenoon Captain Halliard, faithful to his threat, paid me a visit. I was not ready for him then, but I showed him one-half of Cormorin's certificates. They did not abate his persistency for payment of the note, and I promised to pay him at three o'clock in the afternoon, without fail. As I had the money in my pocket, I could safely make the promise.

At the appointed time he presented himself before me.

16

CHAPTER XVII

PROVIDING FOR THE WORST.

"THERE is your money, principal and interest," said I to my uncle, carelessly tossing him the bills. "You have compelled me to sacrifice my coppers, but I am rid of you now."

"Rid of me! It isn't necessary for you to be impudent, Paley," replied the Captain.

"I assure you, it is a very great satisfaction for me to feel that there is now no possible way in which you can annoy me."

"I don't want to annoy you."

"I thought you did. You have been crowding me pretty hard. You have compelled me to pay this note, for no other purpose than to annoy me. You have done your worst, and I hope you are satisfied."

"You may have the money again, if you want it," said he; for, like other bullies, when he felt that his power was gone, he was disposed to make peace.

"I don't want it now. I have sold out my

stock at a loss to gratify your malice. If you can do anything more to crush me, I hope you will do it."

"I don't want to crush you. What are you talking about?" added my uncle, impatiently.

"I don't know what you mean by crowding me so hard, then."

"Paley, you are living too fast. All I have done has been for your good."

"I don't see it; and I don't exactly know by what right you purpose to take the management of my affairs into your own hands. You have an offer for my house, and you have attempted to drive me out of it. Let me say that I would go into bankruptcy, or into the State Prison, before I would submit to any such dictation. I am of age and I think I am able to take care of myself. I hear that Aunt Rachel is better to-day, and is steadily improving. I shall take the first occasion to tell her how you have used me."

"Do you want to make trouble in the family?" asked he, evidently startled by my threat; for the handling of the invalid's property was of some importance even to a gentleman of Captain Halliard's wealth.

"I want justice done, though the heavens fall.

Aunt Rachel never intended that I should be driven up to pay this thousand dollars, as you have done the business."

"I did what I thought was best for you and for her."

"All right; if you are satisfied, I am."

I think my uncle was rather sorry he had crowded me so hard. He had failed to accomplish his purpose of driving me out of my house, and he knew that I had some influence with my aunt. He was disposed to back out, but I was not willing that he should do so. I did not like the idea of having him around me in the capacity of a guardian, prying into my affairs, and listening to every breath of scandal that related to me.

The sharp words I had spoken produced some effect upon him. But it occurred to me that his malice would be dangerous, and I did not deem it prudent to provoke him any farther. He was intimate with Mr. Bristlebach, and his influence might imperil my situation. It would be utter ruin for me to be discharged before I had replaced the sums I had "borrowed." I moderated my wrath, therefore, and refrained from enforcing my threat. My uncle left me, and I was willing to wait until he made the next move.

I remained at the bank until half-past three o'clock, at which time I had agreed to meet Cormorin, at Young's. He was nearly half an hour late, but he came, and I saw by his countenance that every thing had gone well with him. I should say, in the light of subsequent experience, that every thing had gone ill with him, for the successful concealment of guilt, whatever consequences might follow its exposure, is the greatest misfortune that can befall a man, inasmuch as it leads him farther and deeper into crime.

"Five thousand; there are the identical bills you lent me," said Cormorin, as he laid the money upon the table before me. "I'm all right now, and I hope I shall not have occasion to repeat this folly."

"You will make enough by your operation in Ballyhacks to afford you a sufficient capital for future operations."

"That's so. I shall be worth ten or fifteen thousand dollars next week, as sure as I live. I am going to pay what I owe the bank, and then keep square with the world. You have done me a good turn to-day, Glasswood, and I am not one of the kind that forget such things."

"Here are your certificates. I am glad to have

been able to serve you," I replied, as I handed him the papers. "You said something about another company in which a fellow might make a good thing."

"I did — the Bustumup. Its stock's going up just as that of the Ballyhack did."

"What can I have it for?"

"I am interested in this company, and if you take the stock at once you shall have it for twenty, though it went at twenty-two to-day."

"I will take two hundred and fifty shares of it."

"You are sensible," replied Cormorin. "You have the money in your fist, and you can return it in a week or two, and put ten thousand dollars into your pocket."

I had not told Cormorin my secret, and I think he was anxious to have me invest the five thousand dollars, I had taken from the bank, that we might stand on an equal footing. He desired to possess as strong a hold upon me as I had upon him. I was satisfied of the truth of what he had told me in regard to his own "coppers." I had inquired for myself, and I realized that he was making ten if not fifteen thousand dollars by his operation.

I felt compelled to take the step he suggested. I owed my bank three thousand dollars, and while Aunt Rachel was so feeble, I had no hope of obtaining the amount from her. I must do something to save myself from possible exposure. The brilliant example of Cormorin loomed up before me. If he had made a large sum in " coppers," there was no reason why I should not do the same. It was necessary that I should make the effort, and I gave him the five thousand dollars he had just returned to me, to be invested in Bustumups.

" It will be a safe operation, Glasswood," continued Cormorin. " Bustumups are sure to go up."

I did not regard this last expression as one to be taken in the metaphorical sense.

" You have looked into this matter, Cormorin, and of course you understand it. As things now stand, you and I must hang together."

" That's so; count on me for anything you want."

" Thank you. Now won't you have a bottle of champagne with me ? "

"I am much obliged to you, Glasswood, but I can't stop any longer now. I must get your stock for you before four, or it will cost you twenty-five to-morrow."

"You are confident that this is a safe thing for me—are you not?"

"Oh, perfectly confident!" exclaimed he. "If you don't believe in it, don't do it."

"I rely upon your statements, and go in upon the assurance of what you say."

"Of course you must run your own risk. I can only advise you to do what I would do myself."

"That's enough."

He left me to procure the certificates of stock in the Bustumup Company. I was to wait in the private room I had taken until his return. I was alone, and when I began to think what I was doing, I was appalled at the possibility of failure. I was in debt to the bank in the sum of eight thousand dollars. If my investment should go wrong I could not hope to make good the loss. I should be obliged to flee from my wife and my home, and end my days in exile, if I should be so fortunate as to escape without detection. A cold sweat stood on my forehead as I thought of the possibility of discovery, of being arrested even before I supposed any one suspected me, and of being condemned to the State Prison for ten years or more.

I rang the bell, and ordered a bottle of champagne. I drank several glasses of it, and the fumes went to my brain. I felt better. My thoughts began to flow in another direction under the influence of the sparkling fluid. Bustumups would advance every day. In a week or two they would go up to a hundred dollars a share. If they did this, I should make twenty thousand dollars, besides having my capital returned to me. I should be able to pay off the bank, and have seventeen thousand dollars left. My dream of future success was colored with the pinkiest tint of the wine I drank.

I intended to be cautious. If, after my stock had gone up to fifty, there were any signs of a reaction, I would sell, and still make ten thousand dollars. Cormorin was sure the stock would be twenty-five the next day. If it was, I should clear twelve hundred and fifty dollars. But if it only went up to thirty-five in a week, it would enable me to pay off what I owed the bank, and I should be content even with that.

My new friend brought me the coveted shares, and helped me finish the bottle of champagne before me. For some reason or other he declined to punish a second one with me, and we separated. I went home with my shares in my pocket. When the fumes of the champagne passed off, I was uneasy again. I felt that I stood upon the brink of a precipice. If Bustumups went down instead of going up, I was ruined. There was no possible way for me to redeem myself.

Though my uncle knew I was dealing in stocks — or rather took my word for it — and was plunging into a sea of speculation, he did not warn me against it. He had not a word of caution to utter, and probably had no suspicion that I might be tempted to meddle with the funds of the bank. If he had been as solicitous as he pretended to be for my welfare, he would have warned me of the perils of my course. For my own part, my uncle was a mystery to me.

Lilian with the black silk in prospect, was as happy as a queen. In the evening Tom Flynn called. He was hardly seated before Mrs. Oliphant and Bertha made us a call. " Dear ma " appeared to be cured of her evil propensity, probably because another daughter, through my indirect agency, was in a fair way of being disposed of. We had sacred music, and a lively time generally. I was quite satisfied that Tom would, at no distant day, make my wife's sister his bride.

This prospect was quite enough to appease Mrs. Oliphant, and she really looked quite amiable under the indications of this happy event.

Tom escorted Bertha and her mother home at ten o'clock, and the next day the noble fellow told me with a blush, that he did not leave the house on Tremont Street till the clock struck twelve. A question or two from me brought out the fact that they were engaged. I envied Tom — he was so happy. Why should he not be? He owed the bank nothing. He had not soiled his soul by taking what did not belong to him. He was a strictly moral and religious young man. He would have gone without his dinner rather than stay away from the evening prayer-meeting. I say I envied him. I did; and I would have given all the world, had it been mine to give, for his peace of mind.

I could not sleep that night when I went to bed. I got up and drank nearly half a bottle of Smith's old sherry, which stupefied my brain, and gave me the needed rest from the goadings of conscience and the terrors of the future. My fate depended upon the success of the Bustumup Company. If that went down, I might be called at any time to flee from my wife, and wander in fear and trembling as an exile in some strange land. If I was in peril of exposure I could not remain to face the blast of popular condemnation. My pride would not permit me to live where any man could look down upon me with either pity or contempt.

At twelve o'clock, when I run out for a lunch, I found that Bustumups were quoted at twenty-five. This fact assured me, for already I had practically paid off more than one-third of my debt. The stock went a little higher before two o'clock, and my courage was correspondingly increased. I was rather disturbed, however, at the close of the bank, to see my uncle in close conversation with Mr. Bristlebach. I fancied that I was the subject of their remarks, especially as the president cast frequent glances at me. Captain Halliard looked ugly.

I had shown him a portion of the certificates which Cormorin had lent me. He was a shrewd business man, and though he had not objected to the statement that I had saved half my salary, and invested it in stocks, he might well have doubted the truth of it. Perhaps he had been thinking over my affairs, and had come to the conclusion that my assertions were doubtful. On two occasions he had driven me up to the payment of money, and both times I had met the demand.

Cormorin told me that he always ascertained when the directors intended to make an examination. Captain Halliard meant mischief. He intended, at least, to put me in condition to let Aunt Rachel alone. I am confident he did not really believe that I had borrowed any thing of the bank; but probably he wanted to satisfy himself that I did not obtain my ready money from the drawer. As the conversation continued I became alarmed. The President almost invariably left the bank soon after two o'clock. To-day he remained. As he had done once before since I occupied my position, he might examine the condition of the cash department.

I meant to be on the sure side. I ran into the bank where Cormorin was, and told him what I suspected. He promptly offered to help me out, on the same terms that I had performed a similar service for him.

"I want eight thousand, I whispered. "I will return it to-morrow morning."

"Eight thousand!" exclaimed he. "Why, you are only five thousand short.

" Eight," I replied, firmly.

" IIow's that ? "

" I was three thousand short when I made the little arrangement."

" Thunder ! " ejaculated he, impatiently. " Then you are the eagle and I am the lamb."

" We are both honest fellows, and mean to pay all we owe," I replied. " Do you suppose I would have accommodated you, the other day, if I had not been in hot water myself? Of course if I go down, you go with me."

" But the security ? " he asked.

" Two hundred and fifty shares of Bustumups."

" They are worth only six thousand or so."

" But will be worth more than eight in a few days ; you shall have your bills back to-morrow morning, without fail."

I gave him my certificates and he handed me the money ; but he gnashed his teeth as he did so. If I fell, I should drag him down with me.

" Is everything right in your drawer ? " asked Heavyside, the cashier, slyly, of me, when I returned.

" Certainly it is," I replied. " Why do you ask ? "

" Bristlebach is going to look over our accounts and cash this afternoon."

" All right," I answered, carelessly.

I deposited the eight thousand in my drawer, balanced my cash, and put the trunk into the safe. Paying no attention to any one, and especially not to my uncle, I sauntered leisurely out of the bank.

CHAPTER XVIII

BUSTUMUPS AT FIFTY.

BY the ruse in which Cormorin had instructed me, and for which he had furnished the funds, I had provided against any exposure. By this time I was fully satisfied that my uncle was working against me; not that he intended to ruin me, but only to maintain his own power and influence over me. There are men of this stamp in the world, who will punish their best friends when they refuse to be guided by them. Captain Halliard was as jealous of his influence as he was of his money.

As my account with the bank was now square, I had no fear of the investigation which was in progress. Mr. Heavyside, who had never been suspected of even an irregularity, had been so kind as to inform me of the proposed examination. I had in him a good friend, and a mortgage on his future fidelity to me. I should defeat my uncle this time, as I had before, but it was annoying to be subjected to his espionage, though

I could not afford to have a serious quarrel with him.

I went home at about the usual hour. My Bustumups had done so well that I was tolerably light-hearted. Lilian was as joyous as a dream in June. Bertha had been with her all the forenoon, and I heard much in praise of Tom Flynn. We dined, and then I proposed to Lilian that we should ride out into the country. She was glad to go, and we went. On my return home at six o'clock, Biddy handed me a note from Mr. Bristlebach. I recognized his heavy hand-writing, and my blood ceased to flow in its channels. I tore open the envolope. It was simply a request to appear at the bank immediately.

What could it mean? My cash was all right. They could not have discovered the truth. That was simply impossible. If there was any trouble at the present time, Cormorin, and not myself, would be the sufferer. If there had been a discovery of the whole truth, Mr. Bristlebach was not the man to have sent a note to me; he would have sent a constable. I decided to go at once to the bank, for I was satisfied, from the manner in which the message had come, and by the assurance that my cash was all right, that nothing

17

very serious could be charged upon me. I told Lilian I was going down town for an hour, and she did not bother me with any troublesome questions.

On my arrival at the bank I found the president and my uncle in the directors' room. Both of them looked severe, but Captain Halliard did not seem to be so much at his ease as usual. I knew him well enough to be able to read his thoughts, and whatever mischief was brewing he was at the bottom of it.

" Mr. Glasswood, of course you are aware that there is a deficiency in your account? " said Mr. Bristlebach.

"No, sir, I am not aware of it," I replied ; and as I spoke the literal truth, I answered with confidence.

" You are not ? "

" No, sir."

" Did you balance your cash to-day ? "

" I did, sir; and at half-past two it was all right."

" You put a bold face on the matter."

" Certainly I do, sir. I am innocent of the charge, and I can afford to speak the truth."

" Nevertheless, your cash is short."

"It was not short at half-past two to-day," I replied, glancing at my uncle.

He was uneasy, and did not confront me when I gazed at him.

"It is not a large deficiency," added Mr. Bristlebach, "but large enough to demand inquiry."

"May I ask how much you found it short," I inquired.

"Only three hundred dollars."

There may be some mistake—I hope there is," suggested my uncle.

"Who counted the cash?" I asked.

"We counted it together," replied the president. "I wish to add that I do not regard you as a defaulter or any thing of that sort. I sent for you to enable you to explain the matter."

"I have no further explanation to make. I left my cash all right to-day," I added, confidently.

"He is so sure, that I rather think some mistake has been made," added Captain Halliard.

"Probably there has been. Mr. Glasswood, I have had the utmost confidence in you. When I suspected you before, a second examination convinced me of your integrity. I have no doubt it will be so this time."

" I cannot undertake to keep my cash right, if other persons are allowed to go to my drawer," I continued, rather savagely.

" What!" exclaimed my uncle, springing to his feet.

" I said what I meant to say," I replied.

The remark hit just where I intended it should. Mr. Bristlebach and my uncle had been counting my cash. I had left it all right. If the deficiency was insignificant, it was still enough to ruin me. I had already made up my mind how my cash happened to be short. If the president had made the examination himself there would have been no deficiency. Of course I mean to say that Captain Halliard himself had been the author of the mischief. In other words, he had either taken three hundred dollars from my cash, or had falsely reported his count.

Before I ventured to make this violent statement, I put my uncle fairly on trial, and called up all the circumstances of our present relations to testify against him. He was determined to maintain his influence over me, and to prevent me from saying any thing to Aunt Rachel about him. I had refused to give up my house at his bidding, and prevented him from obliging. his friend, Mr. Brentbone. I had roundly reproached him for his conduct to me, and used language which he could not tolerate in any one. I was satisfied that he had a strong motive for desiring to obtain a hold upon me.

A strong motive, however, is not sufficient to explain so dastardly an act as that in which I had dared to implicate my uncle. A man of integrity, simply an honest man, would not be guilty of so vile a deed. Was my uncle capable of such an act? He had procured my situation for me by bringing up a charge against Tom Flynn which both he and I knew was false — one which he himself had disproved as soon as his purpose was accomplished. If he would do one mean thing, he would not halt at another.

He had compelled me to pay the thousand dollars I owed Aunt Rachel, out of sheer malice, and only to put me in a position where he could control me. The mild speech of the president of the bank assured me that I was not to be harshly dealt with; and my uncle gently suggested that there might be a mistake.

"Be careful what you say, Mr. Glasswood," said the president. "Now I'm going out to get a cup of tea; when I come back we will ascertain whether there is a mistake or not.

Mr. Bristlebach left the room. My uncle looked embarrassed, thrust his fingers into his vest pockets, and seemed to be feeling for something. I was tempted to spring upon him, and throw out the contents of those pockets, for I was satisfied that the deficiency in my cash could be accounted for only in that way.

" Paley, you have been speculating in coppers," said he.

" I have ; but that is my business," I replied, roughly.

"I propose to pay the bank the amount your cash is short, and to hush the matter up where it is."

"I don't ask you to do any thing of the sort."

"I am on your bond, and I must do it. No matter about that. I expected, after you told me what you were doing in coppers, to find a deficit of thousands. I was prepared to pay even that, for you are of my own flesh and blood."

" You are very affectionate ! "

"I have succeeded in quieting Mr. Bristlebach."

"I see you have."

" You talk to me as though I had done you an injury instead of a kindness," added he, reproachfully.

"That is what you have done."

"Your cash is three hundred short," said he, putting his hands into his vest pockets again.

Perhaps I was insane under the pressure of his implied charge; at any rate, under the impulse of the moment, without consciously determining to do it, I sprung upon him like a tiger; and having no warning of my purpose myself, I gave him none. I thrust my hands into his vest pockets, and drew from them whatever they contained. I retreated into the farther corner of the room to examine my capture. The deed was done so quick that Captain Halliard had no time to resist, though he seized me by the shoulders. I was furious, and shook him off like a child.

"What do you mean, you villain?" gasped he.

I paid no attention to him, but proceeded to examine my prize. Among other things I found three bills, of one hundred dollars each.

"Do you mean to rob me, Paley?" demanded he; but, like Hamlet's ghost, he appeared to be "more in sorrow than in anger;" and more in fear than in sorrow.

"Do you carry your money in your vest pockets, sir?" I demanded.

"Sometimes I do."

" You took these bills from my trunk when you counted my cash."

" Nonsense, Paley ! "

" I can swear to one of them, at least," I replied, holding up one of the bills, on the face of which some clown had written a sentence about depreciated currency, that had attracted my attention. " I left this bill in my trunk in the vault at half-past two to-day; at half-past six I find it in your pocket."

" Do. you think—"

" I know ! " I interrupted, him, in the most savage manner. " If I can find a policeman, I will put you on the track to the State Prison."

" Don't be absurd, Paley," interposed my uncle; but I saw that there was no heart in the remark. " There must have been a mistake in the counting."

" You stole this money from my trunk to get me into trouble."

" Didn't 'I tell the president that I would pay the deficit ? " asked my uncle. " Hush up! There comes Mr. Bristlebach! Not a word of this to him."

" You confess, then, that you took this money from my trunk ? "

" By-and-by we will talk about it," he replied, with much agitation.

I had proved my case. My uncle was a villain. He had taken three hundred dollars from my cash — not enough to make me look like a defaulter — for the purpose of maintaining his influence over me, and to keep me from telling bad stories about him to Aunt Rachel. Guilty as I was, I made myself believe that I was an innocent man, because I was not guilty in the direction he accused me. Mr. Bristlebach returned to the room.

" I am satisfied, from what Mr. Glasswood says, that there must have been a mistake in our count," said my uncle. " As I told you, I was confident my nephew was honest, but I was fearful, when I learned that he had been speculating in coppers. I thought, as I was on his bond, we had better look into the matter. I am perfectly satisfied now."

This very consistent statement was assented to by the president, but my cash was counted again, at the request of Captain Halliard. I was in doubt whether to restore the three hundred I had wrested from the conspirator, but I concluded that I could not afford to expose him. We counted the cash, which was mostly in large bills, and of course I was fully vindicated. The president was profuse in his apologies, and my uncle was kind enough to take the burden of the blunder on himself. He could even see where he had made the mistake. I left the bank with him, and we walked up the street together.

"That was an awkward mistake of mine," said he.

"Very," I replied, with a sneer.

"But I think I can explain it."

"I don't think you can."

"You seem to have taken it into your head that I mean to injure you."

"I have."

"You are mistaken. I am on your bond. Money is so plenty with you, that I was afraid I might be called upon to pay the bond. Bristlebach is so intimate with me that I could satisfy myself without doing you any harm. That was all I intended."

"And that's the reason why you took three hundred dollars out of my trunk, I suppose?"

"Mr. Bristlebach handed me that money himself. I wanted to pay out that amount to-night, and I drew a check for it. I entirely forgot it

when we counted the cash, and that was the
deficit. Here is the check; as you put the money
back, I took the check from your drawer. That's
the whole story."

" Why didn't you explain it to Mr. Bristlebach,
then ? " I asked, believing not a word he said.

" Because it was so stupid of me to forget that
the check had been paid out of your cash."

 " Very stupid, indeed ! "

"I will tell him about it to-morrow," added
my uncle.

As I have said before, a man in my situation
could not afford to quarrel with one so powerful
as Captain Halliard. I kept my own counsel, not
wholly certain that he would not yet be called
upon to pay the amount of his bond on my account. We parted in peace, and I was abun-
dantly pleased that I had been able to fight off
the charge.

The next morning, when I went to the bank,
I took the eight thousand from the cash, which
Cormorin had lent me, and returned it to him.
He was a happy man then. I doubt whether
he slept a wink the night before, for the idea of
being responsible for my deficit, as well as his
own, could not have been very comforting to
him.

I was all right at the bank, and my uncle treated me with "distinguished consideration." On several occasions he assured me he should use his influence in my favor with Aunt Rachel. If I wished for the money he had compelled me to pay — solely for my own good — he would let me have it again. Indeed, if I was short at any time, he would lend me a thousand dollars. I thought I might have occasion to avail myself of his offer, and I was pleasant and pliable. I said nothing more about the three hundred dollars.

For a week all was well with me. Ballyhacks went up to seventy-five; but Bustumups were slower, and had only touched forty in the same time. This figure satisfied me, inasmuch as it enabled me to pay my debt at the bank. Yet I believed, with the utmost confidence, that there was five or ten thousand more in the stock for me, and as long as things were easy at the bank, I did not think of realizing.

Then I was sick for ten days, and was obliged to stay in the house, but even while my brain was on fire with fever I went down town one day. I dared not leave my deficit to be discovered by my substitute. I compelled poor Cormorin to lend me the eight thousand again, on the security of my Bustumups. They were worth nearly this sum in the market by this time, and he did not object very strenuously.

As soon as I was able to get out, I hastened back to the bank, and took my place at the counter. Cormorin had sold his stock at eighty. Bustumups were quoted at fifty, with a prospect of a further advance. My friend had made thirteen thousand dollars. When I had made him whole, he nstantly resigned his place, fearful, I think, of getting into trouble through my agency. He went to New York, to go into business there. I did not care. My stocks at fifty paid my debt, and left me forty-five hundred surplus. I was excited over the prospect. I should be a rich man in a few weeks.

But everything did not turn out just as I anticipated.

CHAPTER XIX

A CRASH IN COPPERS.

I WAS worth forty-five hundred dollars while Bustumups were quoted at fifty. Every day, while they hung at about this figure, I debated with myself the policy of selling, paying my debt, and investing my surplus in some other concern. Perhaps I should have done so, if I had known of a company in which I could place entire confidence. I missed Cormorin very much, for I needed his advice; and I had come to regard him as an oracle in the matter of coppers.

It looked like madness to sacrifice a stock which might go up to eighty or a hundred, as the Ballyhack had, and though my debt worried me, I could not make up my mind to let it go. If I could put ten thousand dollars in my pocket, my fortune would be made, for with this sum I could operate on a large scale. There was no danger of another examination of my cash at present, and I was secure. But Bustumups did not advance as rapidly as I wished. They hung at about fifty.

I was told that parties were investigating the condition of the mine, and that as soon as they reported, the stock would go up as rapidly as Ballyhack had done. I was willing to wait patiently for a week or two, while the stock about held its own. Its trifling fluctuations up and down troubled me, but the parties who worked it convinced me that these were only accidental changes.

Though I saw my uncle every day, he did not allude to his own villainy, and I was prudent enough to wait until I was out of the woods before I did so. In the course of a couple of weeks, when I had made my ten thousand dollars, I intended to resign my position, and then I could afford to express my mind very freely to Captain Halliard. With ten thousand dollars in my exchequer, I could go into any business that suited me, and make money enough to support me in a style becoming my abilities.

I still had strong hopes that the fortune of Aunt Rachel would be mine. She was now apparently rapidly regaining her health, and I determined to improve my chances as soon as I could. On the following Saturday afternoon I took Lilian down to Springhaven with me, and we both used our best efforts to win her regard. I took her out to ride, I read to her, and the old lady seemed as fond of me as when I was a boy. I was her only nephew, and it had been often reported that I was to be her heir, though on what authority I did not know. I invited her to spend a week or a month at my house in Boston, and she promised to do so as soon as she was able.

A rumor that the parties who were investigating the condition of the mine intended to make a favorable report sent Bustumups to fifty-five, and I was very happy. I was worth nearly six thousand dollars. At the end of another week the stock went up to sixty, and the balance of worldly wealth in my favor was seven thousand dollars. The game was becoming intensely exciting. Another week or so would realize all my hopes. I should be free and safe.

While every thing was in this cheerful condition Aunt Rachel sent for me, and I hastened to Springhaven, for I could not afford to neglect her summons. She was ready to go home with me, and she accompanied me to my house in Needham street. The old lady was a little surprised to find that I lived in elegant style, as she was pleased to express it; but then she regarded the salary I received, which was double what her minister had, as princely in itself. Simple as were her views of social economy, she did not accuse me of extravagance. Lilian understood the matter perfectly, and was all tenderness and devotion.

One morning, after she had been at our house three days, Aunt Rachel asked me if I knew a certain Squire Townsend, a lawyer, whom the old lady had been acquainted with in the early years of her life. I had heard of him. He was an attorney of the old school, and I hoped she intended to make her will while she was thus kindly disposed towards me. She begged me to see the old gentleman, and ask him to call upon her during the forenoon.

" Do you see much of Captain Halliard, Paley?" asked my aunt, as I was going out.

" I see him nearly every day."

" I wonder he has not been up to see me yet," added the old lady.

I did not wonder. I had not taken the trouble to tell him that Aunt Rachel was at my house.

" Do you wish to see him?" I asked.

" Not particularly. He has done considerable business for me."

18

"I know it. He did some for you while you were sick."

"Did he?"

"He made me pay the thousand dollars I borrowed of you."

"What, Captain Halliard!" exclaimed the old lady.

"He did."

"Why, I didn't tell him to do that."

"I know you didn't, but he showed me a power of attorney from you, and I couldn't have helped myself if I had wished to do so; but I paid it, and it's of no consequence now."

"I didn't mean you should pay that money. I shouldn't have cried if you had never paid it. I'll talk with Squire Townsend about it. Couldn't you take care of my property for me just as well as your uncle?"

"Well, I suppose I could," I replied, rather indifferently.

"I never liked your uncle very well. He is too sharp for me. I'll see what can be done."

"I wouldn't say anything about meddling with Captain Halliard, at present," I suggested, for I was somewhat afraid of him myself.

"I'll see about it; but I didn't mean he should

trouble you about that money. He'd no business to do it, and I shall tell him so when I see him."

I did not intend she should see him at present. I went to the office of Squire Townsend, on my way down town, and left a message for him to call upon my aunt. I was fully persuaded in my own mind that she intended to make a will, and that she had come up to Boston in order to have the instrument drawn up by her old friend. Every thing looked rosy to me, for the old lady would certainly leave me the larger portion, if not the whole, of her worldly wealth.

When I went home in the afternoon I learned that Squire Townsend had spent a couple of hours with Aunt Rachel, but Lilian had not heard a word that passed between them. Then the squire had called a carriage, and they had gone off together. I was not very anxious to know where they had gone, though I concluded that it was only to the office of her old friend for the purpose of having the will properly signed and witnessed. Now, as always before, Aunt Rachel kept her own counsel. She never told how much she was worth, or what she intended to do with her property. She was true to her antecedents, and during the remainder of her stay she never mentioned the nature of her business with Squire Townsend, as she invariably called him. She said a good deal about the worthy lawyer's history, and told stories about him at school. She was glad to meet him once more before she left the world, but she did not hint that she had special business with him.

The old lady staid her week out, and then said she must go home. She did not think the city agreed with her. She did not sleep as well nights as at Springhaven. Both Lilian and I pressed her to remain longer, and promised to do every thing we could to make her happy, but she was resolute, and I attended her home, a week to a day from the time she arrived.

I never saw her again.

During the week that Aunt Rachel was with me, Bustumups began to look a little shaky. From sixty the stock went down to fifty-five in one day, but it immediately rallied, and those who managed it assured me it was only because money was a little tight, and a considerable portion of the stock had been forced upon the market. I proposed to sell, as I had promised myself that I would on the first appearance of a decline.

"Don't do it," said the operator. "Wait three

days, and you can take sixty, if not sixty-five, for your stock. If you crowd it upon the market at once, you will drive it down, and cheat yourself out of twelve hundred dollars."

" But it looks shaky," I pleaded.

" The best stocks on the street go up and down by turns. Wait till day after to-morrow, at least."

I did wait, because I did not like to have twenty-five hundred dollars taken out of my pocket at one swoop. Two days after, I was in a fever of anxiety about my Bustumups. They had gone up and down under the influence of various rumors, good and bad, and no one could foresee the end. At noon Tom Flynn went out for his lunch.

" The coppers are in a bad way," said he, taking his place at the counter on his return.

" What is the matter with them ? " I inquired, with my heart in my throat, for my very reputation rested upon the prosperity of the coppers.

" Ballyhacks have dropped down from eighty to fifty," added Tom.

" What ? " I exclaimed.

" That's what they say. Did you own any ? "

" No. no ; no Ballyhacks," I replied, struggling to conceal my emotion.

I had not told Tom I was speculating in coppers, and I think he knew nothing about it, though he might have heard something of the kind.

" Did you own any coppers ? " he inquired, with a tone and look that indicated the sympathy he felt for me.

" None of any consequence," I replied.

I dared not talk with him about the matter lest I should expose my emotion. With the stunning intelligence he had communicated to me on my mind, it was simply impossible for me to discharge my duties in the bank. I could hardly tell a hundred-dollar bill from a thousand. I told the cashier that I was sick, and was fearful that I should faint again if I did not get out in the air. He took my place, and I staggered out into the street. There were people on the sidewalk, but I could not see them. Every thing seemed to be without form or shape. I was in a fearful agony of mind, and dreaded lest I should drop senseless upon the pavement.

I went into a saloon and drank a glass of brandy. I sat down at one of the little tables to gather up my shattered senses. Ruin stared me in the face. If Ballyhacks had fallen from eighty to fifty, what hope could there be for Bustumups ? After all, the mischief might be confined to this particular stock, and mine might be still on the top of the wave. The brandy I had drank seemed to have no effect upon me. I took another glass, and my courage began to rise a little. The saloon was nearly filled with people, and there was a confused jabber of tongues all around me. Men spoke to me, and called me by name. I replied mechanically, but I could not have told a minute later who had spoken to me.

" But they are a fraud," said a gentleman, seating himself at the table next to mine.

" Certainly they are," replied the other. " The Ballyhack mine has produced some copper; but they say there is not a particle of metal on the Bustumup track — not an ounce! The managers of this affair ought to be indicted and sent to the State Prison."

" Merciful Heavens! " I ejaculated to myself, " I am ruined! "

" Ballyhack has gone down to forty within half an hour," added one of the gentlemen.

" I heard a man offer Bustumups just now for twenty, and people laughed at him," added the other. " I don't believe they will bring ten."

" Probably not. There is not a dollar of value

in them. The thing is an unmitigated swindle."

The whole of the savage truth was poured into my ears. A moment later, I heard some one say that the managers of the Bustumup Company had found it convenient to disappear. I was almost a maniac. I cursed my folly because I had not sold my stock when it began to look shaky. The villains who had comforted me and made promises that I should sell at sixty were simply designing knaves, who had fraudulently worked this stock up to sixty, while there was not a penny of real value in it.

The first shock bore heavily upon me, but I soon recovered in some measure from its effect. I went into the street, and inquired for myself, in regard to the coppers. There were two or three substantial companies which were actually producing metal and paying handsome dividends. The other companies were swindles ; and Bustumup was the most egregious humbug of the whole. I tried to get an offer for my stock, and found it would not bring a dollar a share. Indeed, it could not be sold at any price. In a word, the five thousand dollars I had borrowed from the bank was a total loss.

I will not attempt to describe the misery into

which I was so suddenly plunged. If I had sold my stock a week before, I might have paid my debt and had five thousand dollars left. Now I was a defaulter in the sum of eight thousand dollars. It was horrible to think of. There was no possible way, that I could see, to escape the consequences. What should I do?

I went back to the bank and told Mr. Heavyside that I was better. I resumed my place at the counter, and did my work till the bank closed, sustained by the brandy I had drank. I tried to devise some plan by which I could conceal my deficit for a time. I could think of nothing satisfactory. An examination of the affairs of the bank was sure to betray me. I was tempted to commit suicide, as others have done under the same pressure of guilt.

I thought of my wife, and my eyes filled with tears, as I pictured the fall to which she would be subjected. It was ruin to her as well as to me. What would she do, while I was thinking of her in my narrow cell in the State Prison? The thought was madness to me. I swore that this should never be. She should not be the widow of a living man, who could not support her, who could give her nothing but a legacy of disgrace.

My pride rebelled as I thought of being confined in the prisoners' dock, with all my former friends and enemies staring at me. I thought of facing my uncle after he. had been called upon to pay the bond; of meeting Buckleton, Shaytop, and others to whom I had talked so magnificently. I could not survive the crash. I could not live in dread of the calamity that impended. While I was thinking what to do, my uncle came into the bank. He was a cold-blooded wretch, but he was afraid of me.

He began to talk of coppers, as, of course, I expected he would.

CHAPTER XX.

THE LAST STEP.

"I HOPE you are not in very deep, Paley," said Captain Halliard, after he had stated the question in regard to the copper stocks.

"Not very, but I am bitten somewhat," I replied, trying to look cheerful, for I could not think of exhibiting to the enemy the state of my affairs. "Did you own any coppers, uncle?"

"No; not a copper. I had some, but I got rid of them," replied the wily man of the world, rubbing his hands to indicate that he was too shrewd to be involved in any speculation that could possibly miscarry.

"You are fortunate."

"Speculation is just as much a trade as any other branch of human industry. It requires brains, forethought, coolness. Novices should be cautious how they venture beyond their depth, for they are almost sure to be bitten. I am sorry you have been trapped, Paley."

"I'm not badly hurt, though of course the small

loss I have experienced must make some difference in my future arrangements. And, by the way, I should like to avail myself of your kind offer."

" What was that ? " he asked, rather blankly.

" You offered to lend me money if I was short."

" Just so."

" I want a thousand dollars."

" Of course you mean of your aunt's money ? "

" It won't make much difference to me whose money it is, if I only get it."

" You shall have the thousand you paid me on her account."

" Very well, sir."

He gave me his check for the amount, and I wrote a note for it, payable to my aunt. The captain wished to ascertain how much I had lost by the copper explosion, but I evaded a definite answer, and intimated that I was bitten to the extent of only a few hundred dollars. I had now a thousand dollars in my pocket, besides about a hundred in my possession before. I felt a little easier, though the terrible pressure of my load still rested heavily upon me. I am not disposed to moralize in this place upon the guilt of my conduct, for really the guilt at that time did not trouble me half so much as the fear of detection.

I owed the bank eight thousand dollars. I had "tinkered" the books· so as to account for the deficiency, but the record would not bear a very close examination. The fact that I was mixed up in these miserable copper stock speculations was quite enough to excite suspicion, for I could not hope that the fact was unknown to the directors, as long as my uncle knew it. I felt as though I was living on a powder magazine which might explode at any instant. The slightest accident might reveal the whole truth to Mr. Bristlebach.

If I should happen to be sick a day, so that I could not go to the bank, my false entries might be detected. Even while I was in the daily discharge of my duties, the president or the cashier might be tempted to examine my accounts. On the other hand, I might go a year or more without discovery, though the chances were apparently all against me. If I ran the risk of the future, I should live in constant terror of an explosion. The death of Aunt Rachel, I confidently believed, would ·enable me to pay off my debt; and the question was whether or not I should take the chances of detection until the possession of her money enabled me to set myself right with the bank.

My aunt's health was so much improved that I could not reasonably expect to have her money for some time. In a week, a month, a year — but be it sooner or later, it was sure to come — my deficit would be exposed. It might be discovered while I was at home, or at least before I had any suspicion that I was in peril. I should have no time to provide for my own safety. I was liable to be arrested in my own house, without any warning, and then nothing could save me from a term in the State Prison.

The cold sweat dropped from my brow as I thought of this fearful contingency. I should not have a moment for preparation; an opportunity to take the first train departing from the city; or even to hide myself in the dark places of the city. Cold irons on my wrists, a gloomy dungeon for my resting-place, with the loathing and contempt of my fellow-men, were all that would be left to me then. Lilian, whom I loved with all my soul, would be reduced to despair. My savage mother-in-law would not cease to reproach her, as long as my wife was a burden in the maternal home.

I could not face the emergency. I was determined to place myself beyond the possibility of such an awful crash. I was resolved that Lilian, whatever she might think of me, should never be compelled to look in upon her husband through the bars of a prison cell. Before the discovery of the deficit, I could make such arrangements as I pleased. Afterwards, I could do nothing. It seemed to me then that I had not a day or an hour to spare. I had decided to save myself from the consequences of one tremendous error, by plunging into another. Of course I could not flee from Boston with only a thousand dollars in my pocket. I am surprised now when I consider how easy it was for me to think of taking from the bank no less a sum than thirty thousand dollars. I did not now flatter myself that I intended only to borrow the money, though it did occur to me that Aunt Rachel's fortune would in part pay my debt. Before I left the bank that day, I put in my pocket ten thousand dollars, so that if my errors were immediately discovered, I should not be wholly unprovided for.

I went to a broker where I was not known, and bought a thousand pounds in gold, which I carried home in a small valise I purchased for future use. I concealed the gold in my chamber ready for the final move when I should be required to make it. I was intensely excited by the resolution I had taken, and my thoughts seemed to move with tremendous rapidity. I had decided upon the precise plan I intended to follow; but of course it was necessary for me to move with the utmost circumspection.

I had only a day to spare, for we must leave Boston the next evening. I must prepare Lilian for a great change in her future. I must lay my plans so as not to excite a breath of suspicion in any one, especially at the bank. I had hardly twenty-four hours left to complete my arrangements. I composed myself as well as I could, and went down to dinner. Lilian was as cheerful as she always was when I came into the house, and it almost started the tears in my eyes when I thought what she would be if the world knew the whole truth in regard to my affairs.

"Lilian, I have been unfortunate to-day," I began, as a suitable introduction to the plan I had to propose.

"Unfortunate! Dear me! What has happened?" she asked, dropping her pretty chin and her knife and fork at the same time.

"I have lost a good deal of money."

"Lost a good deal of money?"

" Yes, a large amount."

" Why, Paley ! "

" Don't look so sad, Lilian. It won't kill me ; and while I have you, I need not complain."

" But how did you lose it, Paley ? "

" By the fall of stocks."

" I showed her one of the evening papers, in which the bursting of the copper bubble was fully detailed. She looked at the article, but she could not understand it, and I explained the matter to her.

" You haven't lost all—have you, Paley ? "

" No, not all, my dear. But I have something else to tell you. How would you like to live in Paris for a year or two ? "

" In Paris ! " exclaimed she, her face lighting up with pleasure.

" In Paris, Lilian ; and perhaps we may go to other parts of Europe."

" O, I should like it above all things ! I have always thought if I could ever go to Europe, I should be the happiest woman in the world. But what do you mean, Paley ? You surely do not intend to go to Paris?

" I am thinking of it."

" Are you, really ? " she continued, opening her

19

bright eyes so wide that her whole soul seemed to shine out through them.

"I am, truly; but I was thinking you would not be able to go so soon as I should be obliged to leave."

"O, I would go to-night, if I could only go!" she replied, with enthusiasm.

"I have an offer, or a partial offer, from a concern in New York to act as its financial agent in Paris."

"Accept it, Paley — do accept it. I shall be so happy if I can only go to Paris!"

"I don't know certainly that I can have the position, but I am pretty confident that I can."

"Don't refuse it, Paley. As you love me, don't!"

"But there are a great many difficulties in the way," I suggested.

"O, never mind the difficulties!"

"But we must mind them."

"Well, what are they?"

"In the first place we must go to New York to-morrow night."

"We can do that well enough. I am ready to go to-night."

"I can't go and leave this house, and all the

furniture, .paying the rent while I am gone."

" Leave it in the hands of Tom Flynn. He will sell the furniture and let the house. There are enough who will want it."

" That is not even the principal trouble. The bank will not let me off without my giving some notice, so that the officers can get another person in my place."

" It would be mean in them to keep you when you have a good chance to better your condition."

" I think I can manage it somehow, Lilian; and I feel almost sure that we shall go."

" O, I am so glad ! "

" But, Lilian, you must not tell a single soul where you are going, or, indeed, that you are going at all."

" Not tell any one ! Why not ? " she asked, as if it would be a great hardship to deprive herself of the pleasure of telling her friends that she was going to Paris.

" I will tell you why, Lilian. It is difficult and dangerous business. I am not sure of the position yet. Suppose I should go to New York, and then, after I had thrown up my situation in the bank, find that the firm who made the partial offer did not want me? I should have lost my present place without having obtained another."

"That's very true. I understand you, perfectly."

"If I find in New York that I can have the position, it will be time enough for me to resign my place in the bank. If I am disappointed, I have only to return to my present place. If it should get to the ears of Mr. Bristlebach that I am doing anything of this kind, he might fill my place in my absence — don't you see?"

"I do; it is plain enough."

"You can tell your mother that you are going away to-morrow night, and that possibly I may accept a position in New Orleans."

"In New Orleans?"

"Yes; it won't do to say any thing about Paris yet."

"I am sorry we have to go off in this way; but I would rather do it than not go at all."

I am willing to confess that my conscience reproached me for thus deceiving my loving wife; but I believed that I was doing it for her good — to save her from a fate so terrible that neither of us could comprehend it. We discussed the details of the plan in full, and she promised to be as circumspect as I could desire. We had two traveling trunks which we had used upon our bridal tour, and these were immediately brought into requisition. Leaving Lilian to commence packing, I left the house with the intention of seeing Mr. Brentbone, who had so long been anxious to have my house. I found him at his lodgings. I stated my business, and inquired if he still wished to obtain the dwelling.

"I am still open to a trade. I offered your uncle three hundred bonus for the house," said he.

"But I wish to sell my furniture."

"Very well; if it suits my wife, I will buy it."

"I lost a good deal of money to-day by the coppers, and I must change my plans."

"Ah! I am sorry for you; but I see you are a prudent young man."

"I am in a hurry to dispose of the matter, for I have a good chance to board now. If you and Mrs. Brentbone will walk over to the house, we can show you what there is in it."

The gentleman and the lady were willing, and I accompanied them to Needham Street. Mrs. Brentbone found some fault with the furniture, and rather objected to purchasing it. I intimated that I should not dispose of my lease unless I could sell the furniture.

"What do you ask for the furniture?" he inquired.

"Twenty-two hundred dollars, including the piano, or seventeen hundred with out. I can show you bills for fifteen hundred; and a hundred small things not included in them."

"You ask too much. I must pay twenty-five hundred to get possession, at this rate," said Mr. Brentbone. He made me various offers, but I was satisfied that he would give my price, and I did not abate a dollar. The trade was closed, and he agreed to see me at the bank the next day, where we were to pass the papers. My landlord consented to endorse the lease over to the new tenant. Mrs. Brentbone had a talk with Bridget, and engaged her to remain in the place. Everything was going as well as I could expect. Lilian and I staid up till midnight packing our clothes, and preparing for our abrupt departure.

I went to the bank as usual, the next morning. On my way I stopped at the pianoforte warerooms, and bought the piano in my house which I had only hired, for however guilty I had been, and intended to be, I still had a certain sense of worldly honor, which would not permit me to do what I regarded as a mean action, though I acknowledge that I did not discriminate very nicely in some portions of my conduct. But I settled the bill for four hundred dollars.

Mr. Brentbone came according to his promise. I gave him the lease, and the bill of sale of the furniture for his check. My uncle happened to come in while we were doing the business. I told him that my losses the day before had induced me to accept Mr. Brentbone's offer for my house. He commended me for my prudence. Mr. Bristlebach also expressed his approbation of the economical step I had taken, and declared that he had more confidence in me than before. He liked to see a young man take counsel of prudence.

I took advantage of his good-nature to put in my request for leave of absence for a single day, to enable me to visit a friend in Albany who was sick. The permission was promptly granted. I balanced my cash for the last time, leaving it thirty-eight thousand dollars short, to account for which I altered various charges and credits, and made several fictitious entries. The account was left square, and if no particular investigation was instituted, my deficit might remain concealed for some time. With the twenty thousand dollars which I had just appropriated I left the bank— for the last time.

CHAPTER XXI.

AN EXILE FROM HOME.

I WAS astonished to find that I could commit a crime of such magnitude with so little remorse. It is true, the sin had become, in a measure, necessary to my salvation, and that of my wife; but I was only excited, not burdened with guilt, when I did the deed. I had been traveling very rapidly on the downward road, and in a few weeks I had acquired a facility in crime which enabled me to rob the bank of thirty thousand dollars without considering any thing but the peril of being discovered. Fatal facility, which can only be avoided by those who refrain from taking the first step!

I had deluded myself into the belief that principle was only a worldly sense of honor. Tom Flynn was a man of genuine principle, for his actions were based upon a religious foundation, which alone can vitalize principle. A man may be honest because it is safer or more reputable to be so; but then he would steal if it were not for being found out, and will be as dishonest as fashion or custom will tolerate. When I had leisure to think of the matter, I marvelled that I had fallen so easily; and this was the explanation I made to myself.

Tom Flynn had said as much as this to me, in the way of argument, assuring me it was quite impossible for a man without the love of God and the love of man in his heart — which is the epitome of the whole gospel — to have any genuine principle in his soul. Any thing short of this is mere sentiment, which is blown aside by the rude blast of temptation. The hymn he used to sing so much seemed to tell the whole story: —

> " I want a principle within
>   Of jealous, godly fear ;
> A sensibility to sin,
>   A pain to find it near."

Worldly honor, the fear of discovery, the bubble of reputation, are not enough to keep a man in the path of rectitude. But I will not anticipate the reflections which were forced upon me afterwards. I did not believe I was much worse than the majority of young men. I certainly did not mean to steal when I began to take money from the bank; and even when I found it necessary to flee from the anticipated consequences of my errors, I had a certain undefined expectation of being able to restore all I had taken. The fortune of Aunt Rachel still flitted through my mind as the solution of the difficult problem.

I left the bank struggling to look cool and indifferent. I bowed and spoke to my acquaintances as naturally as possible. In two or three hours more I should be out of the city, perhaps never to see it again. I could not even go down to Springhaven to see my mother — probably I had seen her for the last time on earth. My blood seemed like ice as the thought came to my mind. I reflected upon all she had been to me, all she had done for me. The prayers and the hymns she had taught me in my childhood came back to me as though I had learned them but yesterday. I was amazed at my own folly and wickedness. What a blow I was dealing to that mother! When she heard that her only son had fled from his home, steeped in crime, and covered with shame how she would weep! For days months and years she would groan in bitterness of spirit.

What a wretch, what a villain, what an ingrate I was to strike her in this cruel manner! My sense of worldly honor would have revolted at the thought of giving her even the slightest blow with my hand ; but how inconceivably more cruel was the blow I was giving her by my conduct! Could I have sooner realized the anguish which the thought of my. mother would cause me, I think it might have saved me.

I could not make up my mind to doom her who had given me being, who had watched over me in my childhood, who had loved me as none else but God could love me, to such awful agony as the revelation of my crime would cause her. Was there no way to escape? I could restore the thirty thousand dollars. With the proceeds of my house and furniture I could make up three thousand more. I was really, then, only five thousand dollars in debt — the sum which I had lost in copper stocks. The case seemed not so desperate, after all. I could go to Aunt Rachel, tell her, with the genuine penitence I then felt what a wicked deed I had done. She would lend me five thousand dollars, and I could pay all I owed.

My heart leaped with delight as I thought of this remedy. But then there might be some delay Lilian was all ready to start for New York.

It was possible that the deficit might be discovered before I had raised the money. If it were, I was lost. Still farther, if I paid the three thousand dollars in my possession into the bank, I should not have any thing to furnish another house. I should be compelled to board, and very likely the circumstances would drive me back to Mrs. Oliphant's. I shuddered as I considered it.

I thought of my mother again, and had almost resolved to adopt the suggestion of my better nature, when I was tempted to enter a bar-room. I drank a glass of whiskey. The effect of strong drink upon me was to stupefy my faculties and make me reckless. I drank a second and then a third glass, in as many different saloons. I forgot my mother then. I was excited, and pictured to myself the delights of foreign travel.

I am almost sure now, so strong was the tendency upon me, that I should have carried out the suggestion of my higher impulses, if I had not entered the bar-room. The devil of whiskey drove the good resolution, still in its formative state, out of my mind. If the thought of my mother came back to me, I drove it from me. In this frame of mind, I could not think of humiliating myself by confessing my errors even to Aunt Rachel, the most indulgent of women.

I walked up Tremont Street, thinking of the future. The die was cast, and I refused to avail myself of the means of escape which were open to me. It was a sorry day for me when I turned from the road which might have restored me to honor and integrity. As the events proved, it would have been better, and I should have realized more than I anticipated. I had long dreamed of seeing the wonders of the old world, and the prospect of doing so at once had a powerful influence upon me. Within twenty-four hours I should be on board of a steamer bound to Europe; but at the same time I should be an exile from home, from honor and integrity, leaving a ruined name and a blasted reputation behind me.

"How are you, Paley?"

It was Tom Flynn. His voice startled me. I would rather have met any other one than him, for his very looks seemed to reproach me.

"Ah, how do you do, Tom?" I replied, in some confusion.

"So you are going to Albany to-night?" he added.

"Yes; poor Whiting is quite sick?"

"Who?"

"Whiting; don't you know him?"

"No; who is he?"

"I knew him in the city here, and we were cronies."

Whiting was a myth, but I had a facility for lying which helped me through in an emergency.

"I hope you will find him better."

"I'm afraid, it's all up with him; he is probably in consumption."

"I am sorry for him."

"I suppose you knew I had sold my furniture and lease?"

"No!" exclaimed he, opening his eyes.

"Yes. Brentbone takes possession to-night."

"I am sorry for that, for I liked to go there."

"The fact is, I lost heavily for me in coppers, and I can't afford to keep that house any longer."

"One must be prudent," said he, musing. "I was afraid you were going a little too fast. Did you lose much?"

"Considerable, for me."

"If I can do any thing to help you out, Paley, I will, with the greatest pleasure. I never had anything to do with fancy stocks."

"Thank you, Tom. You are fortunate. But I must go along."

"I suppose you are in a hurry, so I will walk along with you. I don't know but you will think me impertinent, Paley, but I don't want to meddle with your business, in a bad sense. I have been thinking that something was going wrong with you."

"With me?" I demanded, not a little startled by this candid revelation. "Going wrong?"

"I had an idea that you were losing money, or that something serious troubled you."

"What makes you think so?" I asked.

"I hardly know; but you seem to act strangely; to be excited or absent-minded. Perhaps you have lost more on coppers than you care to acknowledge?"

"Well, I have lost more than I ought to lose."

"And — excuse me, Paley — but you have been drinking."

"Only a nipper or two for a pain which often vexes me."

"It's a dangerous practice — don't do it, Paley. Better suffer the pain than fall into a bad habit. I'm impudent, I know, but I can't help it. I wouldn't have things go wrong with you for all the world. Are you in debt?"

"Somewhat."

"Let me help you out. With what I have saved myself, and with what came to me from my father's estate, I have about eight thousand dollars. Promise me that you won't drink any more, and I will let you have money enough to help you out of debt."

"What has the drinking to do with it?" I asked, rather vexed at the manner in which he put the question.

"I am always afraid that any man who drinks will become a drunkard. Perhaps it is a superstition; but I can't help it, and you know that the theory is backed up by common experience."

"I don't think I'm in any danger; but I am not exactly willing to be bought up to total abstinence."

"I didn't mean that, Paley. You know how much wine was drank at your party. Never mind that now; we will talk of it at another time. How much do you owe?"

"Five or six thousand."

"So much!" exclaimed he.

"All of that. I lost just five thousand on Bustumups," I replied, desperately.

"I had no idea you were in so deep as that," he added, looking very serious. "But I will not go back on myself. I will lend you every dollar I have rather than permit the world to go

20

wrong with you. We will talk it over when you return from Albany."

We parted at the corner of Needham Street, for he was going to the Oliphants to see Miss Bertha. What could Tom mean? He had observed that something was wrong with me. I was troubled. If he had noticed it, perhaps others had, and it was time for me to be gone. He was a noble fellow, and I knew that he was deeply concerned about me. From his standpoint, I had been gambling in fancy stocks, had lost, and was in imminent peril of becoming a drunkard under the influence of my financial troubles. He wanted to be a brother to me, but I felt humiliated by the view he took of my case. Why should he think I was in danger of becoming a drunkard? It was fanaticism.

He offered to lend me money enough to pay my debts. I could not borrow it of him. I could not place myself under so great an obligation to him. He tendered me the means of making myself square with the bank; but then I should be a beggar, five thousand in debt, instead of travelling like a lord in Europe, with over thirty thousand dollars at my disposal. My pride resented his offer and I did not give it another thought.

Dinner was ready when I went into the house. Lilian had almost worn herself out in getting ready for her departure. She told me she had been at her mother's, and that the whole family were astonished when she told them I had sold out the English basement house. She had informed them that I had an offer in New Orleans, as I had directed her to do; in a word, she had been faithful to my instructions. Before the carriage came for us, Mrs. Oliphant and her two daughters appeared to bid us good-by. I must say that "dear ma" behaved with great propriety on this trying occasion, for it must be remembered that she expected to see no more of Lilian for months, if not for years.

We drove to the railroad station with our two heavy trunks. It was fortunate that neither Tom Flynn nor any one but the Oliphants took it into his head to "see us off," or the quantity of baggage we carried might have provoked inquiry. The train moved out of the station-house, and I felt that I had bade farewell to Boston forever. I had my wife, but I had sundered all ties with every body else.

"I hope we shall not have to come back here again next week," said Lilian, as the train began to increase its speed.

"There is little danger of that," I replied.

I was obliged to admit to myself that I might possibly be brought back by an officer, with irons on my wrists, within a week. I had committed a crime which would condemn me to the State Prison for a long term of years, if discovered — and it could not be long concealed.

"Do you really think we shall go to Europe, Paley?"

"I have hardly a doubt of it."

"Then why didn't you let me tell mother, and not make her think I was going to New Orleans?"

"I told you the reasons, my dear, and I hope you will be satisfied with them," I answered, rather petulantly.

"Don't be cross, Paley."

"I'm not cross."

But the fumes of the whiskey I had drank were nearly evaporated, and I did not feel right. I could not help dreading something which I tried to define. If Tom Flynn had suspected that something was going wrong with me, it was not impossible that Mr. Bristlebach, or Mr. Heavyside, had been equally penetrating in their observations. It was possible that, at this moment, the bank officers were engaged in examining my accounts

and my cash. Any attempt to verify some of my
entries must infallibly expose me.

Even without any suspicions of me, they might,
in looking over my accounts, discover the altered
figures, or the fictitious items. An accident might
betray me. Perhaps the detectives were already
on my track. Telegraphic dispatches to New
York might place officers at the station in that
city ready to arrest me when I arrived. If my
deficit was exposed, it would be impossible for me
to take a foreign-bound steamer. My photograph,
or at least my description, would be in the hands
of all the detectives.

All these reflections, all these fears and misgiv-
ings, are the penalty of crime. I was called to
endure them, as thousands of others have been ;
and those who commit crimes must remember that
these things are " nominated in the bond." But
no telegram preceded me ; no detectives dogged
my steps ; and the bank had no suspicion that
anything was wrong with me. We went to the
Fifth Avenue Hotel on our arrival in the city.

I hastened down town after breakfast, engaged
a state-room in the steamer which sailed at one
o'clock, and procured a letter of credit on London
for three thousand five hundred pounds, payable

to Charles Gaspiller, whose signature I left to be forwarded to the banker. I then went to a barber, and had my beard, except the moustache, shaved off. When I entered the parlor of the hotel, Lilian did not at first recognize me. She was talking to a lady and gentleman — a young married couple — whose acquaintance we had made at breakfast. They intended to sail in the afternoon for Havana. The husband was about my size, and not unlike me. He wore only a moustache, and for this reason I had sacrificed my beard. If any detectives, after a few days, should be disposed to ascertain what had become of me, they would be as likely to follow him to Havana as me to Liverpool. It was well to be prudent and take advantage of circumstances.

CHAPTER XXII

CHARLES GASPILLER.

I HAD avoided writing my name in the register of the hotel, for I did not wish to leave any recorded traces of my presence in the city. It occurred to me that perhaps Lilian had told her name to her new-made friends, but they would soon be in the tropics, and out of the reach of detectives. I regarded myself as very shrewd, and I could not exactly see how it was possible for any one to obtain a trace of me, after the steamer had departed.

I had given my name at the steamer office as Charles Gaspiller, and the money for my bill of exchange was to be drawn in London under this appellation. I don't know how I happened to select this name. It was a French word which probably came back to my memory from my studies at the high school; but I had forgotten its meaning, though I could read French tolerably well. When I came to ascertain its signification, I was not a little surprised to find that it exactly fitted my case, for it means

" to waste, to squander, to lavish." It was entirely by accident that I chose this word, and I certainly should not have done so had I been aware that it covered my case so exactly.

But if I succeeded in concealing my identity from others, I could not hide it from my wife. If I was Mr. Gaspiller, she must of necessity be Mrs. Gaspiller. We were not at all fitted to pass ourselves off as French people, for my pronunciation had been so neglected at school, that I could hardly speak a word of the language with which I was tolerably familiar by the eye. Lilian knew still less of it. I knew that double *l* in French had a liquid sound, and I called the word Gas-pee-ay. It would be singular that I should have a French name, pronounced with a French accent, and yet not be able to speak the language. I was afraid I had made an unpleasant bed for myself. But I determined as soon as I reached Paris to master the language.

How could I have the assurance to tell Lilian that her name was Gaspiller, and not Glasswood. I might convince her that the latter was too commonplace to travel in Europe upon — indeed she was already convinced of that, for she often, in her lively manner, made fun of the cognomen. I could assure her that, while I was not to blame for my name, the word was so inconsistent, absurd and contradictory, that it would subject me to ridicule. It was no part of my purpose to tell her I was a defaulter, an exile from home, a fugitive from justice. It would break her gentle heart. Yet I was not sure that it would not come to this.

After I had completed all my preparations, I was in her presence with my bill of exchange and my passage receipt in my pocket. She was talking with the lady who was going to Havana when I entered. She looked at me, and as soon as she recognized me, she commented merrily upon the change which the loss of my whiskers made in my appearance. She rose from her chair, but her friend talked so fast that she could not at once leave her. I knew how anxious she was to know the final answer of the great banking-house to which I had alluded. Upon that depended the voyage to Europe. As soon as she could decently do so, she tore herself away from her companion, and sat down on the sofa at my side.

"Are you going, Paley, or not?" she asked, with breathless eagerness.

In answer to this inquiry I inadvertently pulled

out the receipt for the passage money, which constituted the ticket. I did not at the moment think that it ran in favor of " Charles Gaspiller," for I was not quite ready to tell her that I had changed my name.

" What is this, Paley? " she asked, blankly. " I don't understand it."

" Don't you, my dear? Why, it is our ticket for a passage in the steamer to Liverpool," I replied, cheerfully.

" This? 'Received of Charles Gas-pill-er!'" said she, reading just what the letters of my new name spelled.

How stupid I was! Why had I not told her in so many words, that we were to go, instead of doing the thing in this sensational way?

" Precisely so; that is the French for Glasswood," I replied, laughing as gaily as my confusion would permit. " I don't want Frenchmen in Paris to call me *Bois de Verre*, which means wood made of glass, or anything of that sort. The name is Gas-pee-ay, and not Gas-pill-er."

" But how does it happen that the receipt is given to you under this name? "

" Because I don't want to be called Glasswood in Europe. But, my dear, we have no time to spare now, and we shall have ten days of idleness as soon as the steamer sails. So we must not stop to discuss this matter at the present time. We must be on board at half-past twelve, and it is after eleven now," I continued, with sufficient excitement in my manner to change the current of her thoughts.

"Then we are really going!" exclaimed she, opening her bright eyes.

"Certainly we are ; and going immediately."

"Why, I wanted to go shopping in New York, if we were really going."

"Shopping! That's absurd! Ladies never go shopping in New York, when they are on their way to Paris."

"But I must write a letter to mother."

"Certainly ; you have time to do that while I speak for a carriage and pay the bill."

I procured note paper and envelopes for her, and went down to settle my account at the office. The polite book-keeper asked me to indicate the name on the register. I told him I had not written it. I had wound my handkerchief around my right hand, which I held up to him, and declared that I was unable to use a pen. He was kind enough to offer to render me the service himself.

" C. Gaspiller," I added, when he was ready to write.

" What is it, sir ? "

" C. Gaspiller."

He wrote " C. Caspeare," and I was entirely satisfied.

" Three dollars, Mr. Caspeare," said he ; and I gave him the amount, though it was one dollar more than the regular charge.

I was confident that I was leaving no trace of myself here. A carriage was ordered for me, and my trunks were loaded. I went up for Lilian, and found that she had finished her letter. She gave it to me to be stamped and mailed. I took a stamp from my porte-monnaie, carefully adjusted it upon the envelope, and put the letter in my pocket. Of course I was not stupid enough to mail it, since it would betray my secret to those who could not see the necessity of keeping it.

" This is very sudden, Paley," said Lilian, as the carriage drove off.

" Sudden ? Why, I told you this was the way it would have to be done, if it was done at all," I replied.

" I know you did. Won't dear ma be astonished when she reads my letter ? "

" Probably she will be," I answered ; but I thought she would be astonished, long before she read it.

I confess that my conscience reproached me when I thought of the letter in my pocket, and of the deception towards my wife, of which I was guilty. Her father, mother and sisters would wonder, and be permitted to wonder, for weeks if not for months, that they did not hear from her. It was cruel for me to deceive Lilian, and to subject her family to all the anxiety to which I thus doomed them, but I believed that it was a stern necessity, and I silenced the upbraidings of the inward monitor. With thirty thousand dollars of stolen money in my pocket, it may be supposed that I did not trouble myself much upon such an insignificant matter as the peace of my wife's friends.

We went on board of the steamer and I found our state-room. Being one of the last engaged, it was not the best on board, though it was a very comfortable one. Lilian was delighted with it, and declared that she should be as happy as a queen in it. I was afraid she was mistaken. She had never traveled any except on our bridal tour, and I expected she would be sea-sick all the way.

But now she was excited by the prospect before her, and by the busy scene which surrounded us. The steamer was crowded with those who were going, and with their friends who had come to see them off. There was no one to say adieu to Lilian or to me.

If, of the multitude on the wharf, there was any one who felt an interest in me, it could only be a detective. I was a fugitive, and I felt like one. While Lilian was full of life and animated by the scene, I could not help feeling depressed. I was bidding farewell to my native land, perhaps forever. It might never be safe for me to return. I could not get rid of a certain sense of insecurity. It seemed to me, after I saw the men casting off the huge hawsers that held the ship to the pier, that those infernal detectives must come on board and hurry me back to a prison cell in the city from which I had fled.

Any flurry in the crowd, the arrival of a belated passenger, gave me a pang of anxiety which I cannot describe. It was only when the huge steamer was clear of the dock, and the great wheels began to turn, that I dared to breathe in a natural manner. Even then I was thrown into a fresh agony, when a steam-tug came out to us to put the mails on board. I was sure, until it was alongside, that it had been specially chartered by the detectives to arrest me. I was determined to jump overboard and perish in the waves, in sight of my wife, rather than be borne back to a long term of imprisonment in a dungeon. It was better to die than confront my friends in Boston.

I asked one of the officers what the tug was, as she came alongside, that I need not be tempted to do a deed for which there was no real necessity. He assured me it contained only the mails, and I breathed easier; but I was not entirely satisfied that the officers had not availed themselves of this last opportunity to arrest their victim, until the tug had cast off, and the steamer started on her long voyage. I was safe then. My throbbing heart returned to its natural pulsations.

But I could not forget the ruin and disgrace which would soon cover my name and fame in Boston. I could not shut out from my view the horror of my mother when she learned that I was a fugitive from justice, and that I had mocked her fondest hopes. I was miserable for the time, and Lilian rallied me upon my gloomy appearance. There was a remedy which I had tried before for this mental suffering. Leaving my wife for a moment, I went down to the steward's room, and drank a glass of whiskey. I found that lunch was on the table, and I conducted Lilian to the saloon. I ordered a bottle of sherry, and a few glasses of this, in addition to what I had already taken, soon gave my reproaches of conscience to the winds for the time.

I do not intend to describe our voyage. It was an unusually pleasant one, and Lilian suffered but very little from sea-sickness. In a few days, as the distance from my native land increased, I felt tolerably secure from the consequences of my crime; but I found it impossible to get rid of the thought of my mother and other friends at home. Even whiskey and wine soon failed to stupefy me unless I partook of them in inordinate quantities. Lilian told me I drank too much, and begged me not to do so any more. She was so gentle and so tender that I could not refuse, for I had not acquired a decided appetite for the intoxicating cup. I only drank it for the solace it afforded me, and I was fully convinced that the severe headaches and the disordered stomach which troubled me were the effects of this excess. I would gladly refrain, but there was "no peace for the wicked."

I will not attempt to describe my sufferings, though I appeared cheerful and happy to my wife. I could not wholly conceal them from her, and she worried me with her questions, anxious to know what ailed me. We arrived at Liverpool and hastened on to London, for I wished to cash my bill before it was possible for anything to go wrong. I had no trouble in doing so. My signature had already reached the bankers, having come out in the same steamer with me. With the gold which I had brought, I had four thousand five hundred pounds. To prevent any trace being had of me, I went to another banker and purchased a circular letter of credit for a thousand pounds, investing the rest in securities which paid me about five per cent.

We spent a month in London, seeing the sights, and Lilian was as happy as a woman could be. I had satisfied her that the change of name was purely a matter of convenience, and she soon became accustomed to it. She wrote letters to her mother and other friends, and gave them to me to be mailed. I lighted my cigar with them. We had rooms at Morley's, but we saw no one, knew no one in the house, except the servants. One day, after dinner, I went out to obtain some

21

tickets to visit Windsor castle, leaving Lilian in the room. When I came back I found her in terrible excitement. She had a Boston newspaper in her hand, which the landlord, as a special favor, had sent up to our apartments.

" O Charles — Paley ! " said she ; and I saw that she had been weeping. " What does this mean ? "

" What, my dear ? " I asked, appalled at the tempest which was rising.

" This paper says there is a rumor of a defalcation in the Forty-Ninth National Bank, and that the paying teller has disappeared. Were not you the paying teller, Paley ? "

She suddenly ceased to call me Charles, as I had instructed her to do. Evidently she knew more than I wished her to know. I took the newspaper. It was dated about a week after our departure from Boston. The paragraph said it was rumored that there was a heavy defalcation in the Forty-Ninth. The paying teller had been missing for a week. That was all. It was merely an item which some industrious reporter had picked up ; and the particulars had not yet been published. Doubtless the detectives were looking for me.

With tears in her eyes Lilian again demanded an explanation of the paragraph. What could I say?

CHAPTER XXIII

MY CONFESSION.

I HAD apparently deceived my wife as far as it was possible for me to do so. If I told her the truth, would she not spurn me, cast me out and despise me? How could she do less? She was innocent, she was true, she was beautiful; and I was afraid of her. Many and many a time had I cursed my folly and wickedness in departing, even for a moment, from the straight path of rectitude. I wondered that I had been able to delude myself into the belief that taking even a few hundred dollars for a brief period was not a crime.

Be warned, O young man, against the *first* wrong step. While you cheat others, you are the greatest dupe yourself.

In the excitement of seeing the wonders of London I had found some relief from the goadings of conscience, and from the terrors of the future. Almost every day I met some Americans, seeing the sights which attracted strangers. I avoided them, for I feared that I should be recognized by some one from Boston. Lilian desired to see these Americans, but I was obliged to lead her away from them. I was not only an exile from home, but I felt like a leper among my own countrymen.

I was now to face a genuine trial, not a fear, but a reality. After reading the paragraph in the newspaper, my wife had evidently measured my conduct by the suspicions she entertained. By this time she was satisfied that I had not resorted to so much concealment in leaving Boston for the reasons I had alleged. My course was inconsistent from beginning to end. I could easily imagine what had passed through her mind since she read that paragraph.

Possibly I might succeed in lulling her suspicions for the time. I might even argue her out of them. She was innocence and simplicity, like her father, rather than her mother, and would try to believe what I told her. But what was the use to attempt to deceive her any longer? The truth would soon dawn upon her. Yet I had not the courage to be candid with her.

"Why don't you tell me about it, Paley?" repeated she, anxiously, as I turned over the newspaper.

" What shall I tell you, Lilian ? "

" Tell me that you are not a defaulter."

" Well, I'm not, then," I replied, with a smile, which I am sure was a very grim one.

She looked at me, and I saw her eyes fill with tears after she had gazed at me in silence for a moment. I think that my tone and my looks belied my speech, and without heeding the value of the words I used, they conveyed to her the impression that I was guilty.

" Why do you cry, Lilian ? " I asked, moved by her tears.

" I don't know. I can't help it. I feel just as though something was going wrong," she replied, covering her face with her handkerchief.

" Why, what do you mean, Lilian ? "

" Every thing looks very strange to me."

" What looks strange ? "

" That we should have left so suddenly ; that I could not even tell dear ma where we were going ; that you were in such a hurry to reach your new place in Paris, though we have stopped a whole month in London. What is the reason I have no letters from home ? "

" Because none have come, I suppose. I have not received any," I answered, struggling to be funny.

" Paley, you told me, if you left for Paris, that you should write to the bank officers, and resign your situation. You did not do so. This paper says you have been missing for a week, and there is a suspicion that your accounts are not all right. Tell me the worst, Paley. I will try to bear it," she continued, wiping away the tears which filled her eyes.

I was tempted to do so. She had been worrying for weeks about her letters, and she would continue to do so as long as we remained in Europe. No letters would come; none could come. Her parents and her sisters were as anxious about her as she was about them. I could never make peace on the plan which I had laid out at home. My wife would become more and more unhappy, and after the facts of my defalcation had been fully published, I should be still more in dread of meeting some American who would recognize me. As a teller in the bank I was well known to many of the wealthiest men of Boston. Under existing treaties, I could be arrested in most of the European nations, and sent back to the scene of my crime. There was no place of safety for me. I could not flee from the wrath to come.

" What do you suspect, Lilian ? " I inquired.

"I should not suspect anything, if this paper did not say that your accounts were supposed to be wrong. I don't know any thing about such things, but this paragraph set me to thinking how strange your movements were when you left Boston. I wish I could believe it is all right. Why don't you go to your place in Paris? We had to leave home at twenty-four hours' notice, because there must be no delay."

"We are going next week."

"But you have laid your plans to travel in Europe for the next year, at least."

What was the use for me to attempt to explain? It was worse than folly. I had told Lilian so many stories, without regard to their consistency, that she knew not what to believe. I was disgusted with myself.

"I don't see where you got so much money, either, Paley," she added.

"Do you think I stole it?" I asked, somewhat severely.

"I'm afraid you did," she answered, with a shudder.

"You are?"

"When I think of it, I am really afraid you did. Here we are in London under an assumed name. All your papers call you Charles Gaspiller. You told me you had over thirty thousand dollars too."

" I should have had more if I had not lost any," I replied, in rather a surly tone.

" Tell me the whole truth, Paley. Let me know the worst. If my husband is a — "

" A what ? "

" A defaulter, a thief. Let me know it," said she, with a burst of agony.

" A thief ! " I exclaimed, springing to my feet.

" Don't be angry, Paley."

" When my wife calls me a thief, we have been together long enough," I added, sternly.

I took my hat, and rushed out of the room. I was angry, but my wrath was of only a moment's duration. I went out into the Strand, and walked at a furious pace till I reached the American Agency. I wished to know the worst. If I had been published as a defaulter in Boston, I was no longer safe in London. I wished to see a file of Boston papers. I had not thought of looking at them before, because I desired to banish my native land from my mind.

I turned the folios till I came to the one which Lilian had seen. I read the paragraph again. It was very vague. It did not say that the missing teller was a defaulter; it only hinted at something of the kind, for the inference always is, when a bank officer disappears, that his cash is short. I turned over the sheet to find something more about the matter. There was nothing else about me or the bank; but as I examined the paper, my eyes rested for a moment on the list of deaths.

"In Springhaven, 15th inst., Miss Rachel Glasswood, 67 years."

My aunt had passed away on the very day that I sailed from New York! How I cursed myself again and again! If I had not fled I should certainly have been able to pay my debt to the bank in a short time, for I was confident she had left me enough for this. I had banished myself from home for nothing. I had suffered tortures which no innocent man can understand or conceive of, and years of misery were still before me. I had made up my mind long before, that honesty was the best policy; and I even had a glimmering conception of something higher than this. I was sure I should have been happier with poverty and hard labor for my lot, if I could only have been honest.

How I envied Tom Flynn! His piety, which I

had derided, seemed to me now to be the sum total of earthly joy. I do not believe in cant of any kind, but if ever a man was convicted of sin, I was, though I had not yet the courage to attempt to retrace my steps. My wife virtually called me a thief. It was only the truth ; I deserved the epithet, and more than that.

I turned to the next paper. There was nothing about me or the bank in it, and I continued my search till, in a subsequent issue, I found another paragraph. The writer was happy to assure the public that the bank would not lose a dollar by the missing teller. I was surprised at this announcement, for I was indebted to the bank in the sum of thirty-eight thousand dollars. I could not understand it. I turned to the stock lists in the several papers. The shares in the Forty-Ninth had been affected by the first paragraph, but the quotations showed that they had been restored by the information contained in the second.

I concluded that the bank had determined to conceal my deficit to avoid the loss of public confidence. But while I was trying to satisfy myself with this theory, a better one was suggested to me. My aunt died on the day of my departure.

Within the week the substance of her will was known to Captain Halliard. She had left her whole fortune to me, and it was to be used in making good the deficiency in my cash. Of course I had no idea how much she had left, but I supposed it was enough to satisfy the bank, or to pay the loss with the sums for which my bondsmen were liable. One thing was plain, that, if the bank acknowledged no loss, it would not proceed against me; and I realized that I was safe from arrest while in Europe.

I could find no further allusion to the missing teller in any of the papers. If the deficit was made good, doubtless my friends would labor to cover up my errors. As the matter now stood, the money in my possession belonged to me. I tried to make myself believe that it was Aunt Rachel's fortune. But I could not wink out of sight my blasted reputation, for, whatever the papers said, or failed to say, people would have their own opinions about my sudden departure. I was far from satisfied. If my financial record were explained away, I could not get rid of the consciousness of my own guilt, which was positive suffering to me. I was convicted of my sin, and I had even prayed to God for mercy under my misery.

Poor Lilian was suffering quite as severely. I had left her in anger, and the tears came to my eyes when I thought of her. I hastened back to the hotel. I found her lying upon the sofa, sobbing like a child. I raised her in my arms, kissed her tenderly, and begged her to forgive my harsh conduct.

"O, Paley! how miserable I am! Only tell me that you are not guilty, and I shall be happy," she said.

"You would hate and despise me if I told you the truth, Lilian," I replied.

"Then it is the truth!" she exclaimed, springing up, and looking at me with something like horror in her expression.

I did not know what had come over me, unless it was the conscious conviction of my sin, but without definitely resolving to tell the truth, I found it impossible to utter any more lies. Life seemed to me a more solemn thing than ever before.

"I deserve the worst you can say of me, Lilian."

"Then you are a defaulter, Paley?"

"I am; but no one knows it."

"Yes, I know it."

" I wish I could hide it from myself. You shall know all, Lilian."

" But give back the money. I would rather be a beggar and sweep the crossings of the streets, than live in luxury on stolen money."

" Do not be too severe, Lilian. The bank will not lose a dollar by me. On the very day that we sailed from New York, Aunt Rachel died. I have no doubt that she left most of her property to me; and the bank has by this time been paid every dollar I owed it."

" That is some comfort, but not much. You have ruined your reputation. Poor Aunt Rachel! I wish I had seen more of her. What could tempt you to go astray, Paley ? " continued my wife, the tears coming to her eyes again.

" I was extravagant, and lived beyond my means. I borrowed the money to furnish our house, and I was otherwise in debt."

" Why didn't you tell me, Paley? We all thought you were made of money."

" I had not the courage to tell you."

" I know I am giddy, and fond of dress and show, but I would rather have lived in an attic, and dressed in calico, than had you run in debt. You always said you had plenty of money, and your salary seemed to be more than enough to supply all our wants."

"I was weak and foolish, Lilian. I can see it now; I could not see it then."

I told her the whole story from the beginning to the end — how I had been thorned by my uncle and by other creditors, and how I had been tempted to take the money from the bank. I told the truth, as I understood it at the time, when I declared that I had not, at first, intended to rob my employers. She listened to me with the deepest interest, occasionally interrupting me with questions. I told her the whole truth. I did not even conceal from her the fact that I had destroyed her letters. She wept bitterly as she rehearsed the sufferings of her parents and sisters.

"Let us go home, Paley," said she, when I had finished the loathsome confession. "I don't want to see Europe till you have atoned for your fault."

"I may be thrown into prison if I go to Boston again," I suggested.

She clasped me in her arms and wept upon my neck. If her heart was bursting, mine was hardly less affected. The afternoon, the evening, the night passed away, and still we wept and groaned in bitterness of spirit in each other's arms. The clock struck four in the morning before we could decide what to do. She could not advise me to go home if a prison cell awaited me. I never realized the pressure of guilt so heavily before. I never knew my wife till then. Guilty as I was she still clung to me, and was willing to share my lot of shame and disgrace.

In the morning hours I told her what I would do. I would write to Tom Flynn. I would confess my error to him, assure him of the sincere penitence I felt, and be governed by his advice. I did write, page after page, and sheet after sheet, till I had told the whole story. I assured him every penny the bank or my bondsmen had lost should be paid. I would give up everything I had.

I sent my long letter, with another from Lilian to her friends, by the next mail, and anxiously waited a reply, which could not reach me under three weeks.

CHAPTER XXIV

AUNT RACHEL'S WILL.

BOTH Lilian and myself were miserable while we waited for an answer from Tom Flynn. I pictured to myself the surprise of the noble fellow when he read my letter. I was not worthy of the disinterested friendship he had extended to me, but I did not believe that he would spurn me, as I deserved, in my guilt and shame.

We were tired of London, and rather to seek relief from the misery that preyed upon us than to see the sights, we went over to Paris. There was no peace for me in the gay capital, any more than in England, and at the end of a fortnight we returned to London. I had written to Tom that his answer would find me there. I wished him to inform me whether I could safely return to Boston, for I wished to go there, settle up my business, and then begin life anew in some part of the country where I was not known. The future, therefore, was still a problem to me. My first duty was to pay all that I owed the bank.

With the ill-gotten wealth I had with me, and with what Aunt Rachel had left me, if she had left me anything, I should be able to discharge all my obligations.

I felt that I deserved a term in the State Prison, but I was not willing to endure the penalty of my crime. I hoped that I might be permitted to escape if I saved the bank from loss. This settlement was now the question above all others with me, and I looked more earnestly for an opportunity to restore my stolen plunder than I ever had to obtain it. Perhaps if Lilian had not been possessed of my secret I should have felt differently. As it was, she suffered not so much from the fear of what the world would say, as from actual consciousness of my guilt. She had vastly more of real principle than I ever gave her credit for. I had measured her by the standard of her mother, rather than her father. I could not persist in a crime which she so sincerely condemned.

My wife saved me.

The misery which I had suffered before she knew of my guilt was the fear of consequences, the fear of discovery. Her anguish rebuked me. She loved me, even while she despised me for my sin. Day after day we talked of the matter, and

I was more and more impressed with the folly and wickedness of my past conduct. A man is a fool to commit a crime.

The three weeks expired, and I looked for my letter from Tom Flynn. It did not come, but I was willing to believe that there was some unavoidable delay. Tom would certainly write. Another week elapsed. I saw by the morning paper that the steamer had passed Cape Clear, and I waited with intense anxiety for the arrival of the mail, which was due in the evening. Lilian and I sat in the parlor awaiting the postman. There was a knock at the door. The letter had come at last, and I hastened to open the door.

Instead of a servant with the letter, at the door stood Tom Flynn!

" Paley, how are you? " exclaimed he, grasping both my hands.

The tears stood in my eyes, for it seemed like the days of innocence to be thus warmly greeted by him. I could not speak. I threw myself on the sofa and wept like a child.

" Lilian, how do you do? " cried Tom, entering the room, and grasping the hand of my wife.

Poor Lilian! It was more than she could bear. She had no burden of guilt on her pure soul, but she bore mine as though it had been her own. She burst into tears, dropped into her chair, and covered her face with her hands. She sobbed like an infant.

"Come, Paley, don't take it too hardly," said the generous Tom, clapping me on the shoulder. "I received your letter, and of course I know all about it."

"Tom, I'm the most miserable fellow in the world," I said, venturing to look up at him.

"To be candid, Paley, I don't wonder at it. You deserve it. But I rejoice to know that you have come to take a right view of your past conduct," replied he, with the candor which always distinguished him.

"I deserve all the reproaches you can heap upon me. You need not spare me, Tom."

"It is not for me to reproach you, Paley; and I will not. I know how much you must have suffered since you came to yourself."

"You are pure-minded and innocent, Tom; and you can form no idea of it."

"If you repent of your error, Paley —"

"I do repent, and I have asked my God to forgive me."

"Give me your hand, Paley. Let us not say

another word about it. All shall yet be well with you, if you have made your peace with God," said Tom, as he took my hand and pressed it warmly.

" You are too kind, Tom."

" But I am talking here while my wife is wait-ing for me," added he.

" Your wife ! "

" Yes," replied he, with a smile which expressed the pleasure he felt at being able to use the endearing term.

" Where is she ? " asked Lilian.

" Down stairs ; I will bring her up at once."

" But stop, Tom," interposed Lilian, with no little embarrassment in her manner.

" What, Lilian ? "

" Who is she ? " asked my wife, timidly.

" Who is she ? " exclaimed Tom, opening his eyes, and then laughing merrily.

" It seems like an age since I left Boston, and I did not know but you had changed your mind."

" An age ! Why, it is only three months. My wife, of course, is no other than Bertha. We were talking seriously of marriage before you came away. We had fixed the time when I received your letter, but we made it two weeks earlier, so that we could take our bridal tour across the Atlantic. I desired to see you because I could not write you what I wanted to say."

"You are more than a brother to me."

"Wait till I bring Bertha up, before you say anything more.' O, by the way, she knows nothing at all about this affair with the bank. Don't say anything to her about it. It would only make her miserable for nothing. Besides, everything is all right with you, Paley. It is, upon my word."

"How can we conceal it from her?" asked Lilian, as Tom left the room.

"We must do it, since he desires it," I replied. "He says it is all right with me, and if Bertha don't know any thing about my conduct, I suppose others do not."

In a moment Tom appeared with his wife, who rushed into Lilian's arms. They kissed each other, and I think Bertha was the happiest being I ever saw. My wife had not written anything about my crime to her friends, because she feared to compromise me.

"Why didn't you write to us before, Lilian?" demanded Bertha.

"I did, but my letters did not reach you, it seems," replied my wife; and I saw that she shuddered at the deception she was compelled to use.

"We thought you had gone to New Orleans."

"No, we did not; but how is dear ma, and father and Ellen?"

"All very well; and very happy, after they had heard from you. You are a rich man's wife now, Lilian, and I hope — "

"Come, Paley, I must look after my luggage," interposed Tom, who evidently did not care to have me hear what his wife had to say.

I was somewhat astonished to hear Bertha call Lilian a rich man's wife. I could not fully comprehend it. I suppose from this that Aunt Rachel had actually left me her property, as I had anticipated she would, but the most that I had ever heard her rated at was thirty thousand dollars, and according to the city standard, this would not make a very rich man. I was willing to wait for an explanation, however, and I followed Tom out of the room. We went down to the office, where rooms for the newly married couple were secured near mine. The baggage was sent up, and Tom and I took the parlor for a conference.

"I suppose you are anxious to know how your affairs stand in Boston, Paley," said my friend.

"I am only anxious to make my peace with God and man," I replied, earnestly. "I have sinned against God and man. I am a wretch."

"That's a fact, Paley; I can't deny it. But repent and sin no more."

"Tom, if it were not for my wife, I feel that I should be willing to serve out my term in the State Prison. I feel that I have no right to be exempted from the consequences of my crime; but Lilian would suffer more than I should, if the law were to take its course."

"Never mind the law. You must suffer the penalty of God's law — you need not fear man's. When you left, Paley, I took your place. I soon discovered what you had done to your books. I had nearly fainted away when I found what you had been doing. There was a deficit of something like twenty thousand dollars."

"Just thirty-eight thousand, Tom," I interposed.

"Then you were more ingenious than I took you to be," added he, with evident disgust.

"I am going to tell the truth."

"Well, no one has investigated the matter very closely. Indeed, no one knows anything about it but your uncle, Mr. Bristlebach, and myself; not even the cashier."

"That's very strange," I replied, wondering at the secrecy with which the affair had been managed.

" I don't know that it is. You wrote me that you had learned of your aunt's death. She died on the day after you left home. Your uncle telegraphed to you in Albany, but was unable to ascertain where you were. The funeral was deferred as long as possible for you, but you did not return. Before your aunt was buried, I discovered what you had been doing, and realized that you did not intend to return. I told your uncle, and the president what I had ascertained, and we examined the books. Captain Halliard cursed and swore like a madman, but after a while he cooled off, and declared that the news would kill your mother.

" Mr. Bristlebach only added that the news would injure the bank, and it would take a year to convince the public that it had lost only twenty thousand dollars; for that was what the deficit appeared to be then, though the rest of it would have soon become apparent, as the foreign accounts were settled. It was therefore decided to say nothing about it. After your aunt's funeral, Squire — an old lawyer in Court Street, I forget his name — "

" Squire Townsend."

"Squire Townsend came to the bank and told your uncle he had your aunt's will, and that, after paying out a few small legacies, her property was all left to you. This information settled the matter. If you had property enough, the bank would lose nothing by you. Your disappearance called forth a paragraph or two in the papers, but Mr. Bristlebach caused others to be inserted to the effect that the bank would not lose a dollar by your absence."

"I saw all these items."

"So you wrote me. Now, Paley, how much do you suppose your aunt left?"

"I don't know. People used to say she was worth about twenty thousand dollars, but finally the sum got up to thirty thousand," I replied.

"Both were below the fact. Her inventory amounts to over fifty thousand. They say she had twenty thousand more than fifteen years ago. She has never spent much of anything, and her stocks paid her from six to twenty per cent. In a word, Paley, you are a rich man."

I was astonished at this information, and more than ever conscious of the folly of my past conduct.

"You can return to Boston, and if any body

ever suspected that you were a defaulter, your money will cover up the error."

"I don't deserve this good fortune, Tom."

"That's very true," replied Tom, drily. "If you are honest and true, you may enjoy it. I hope it will not undo your reformation."

"It will not, Tom," I added, solemnly. "I am grateful to God for His mercy in sparing me from the consequences of my errors; and I promise you that I will try to be faithful to Him and to my fellow-creatures."

Before I could fully comprehend his purpose, Tom had gently drawn me upon my knees at his side, on the floor, and there he prayed for me more earnestly than I could have uttered the petition for myself. I felt better. The prayer did me good. We talked for half an hour of the religious aspect of my case, and I came to believe that I was a true convert.

"How did they explain my absence?" I asked, as we rose to join our wives.

"Your wife's mother said you had gone to New Orleans to take a situation in a banking office. Your uncle sent a messenger there to find you. We all supposed you were there till I received your letter. I showed it to Captain Hal-

liard, and explained my plan to him. He approved
it, for the executor is waiting for you to claim
your aunt's property."

" I must return immediately."

" No ; I am going to stay over here two or
three months, for I have given up my place in
the bank."

" What is that for ? "

" I have a chance to go into business in the
spring. My old employer in the dry goods business wants to sell out to me for forty thousand
dollars. If you will go in with me, with a part
of your capital, we can make a good thing of it."

" Will you trust me, Tom ? " I inquired, wondering at the confidence he proposed to give me,
after what I had done.

" Paley, I believe your repentance is sincere ;
and believing so, I think you are not so likely to
go astray as you would be if you had had no
bitter experience to remind you that the way of
the transgressor is hard."

" I hope to prove worthy of your confidence
and regard, Tom." I replied, clasping his hand.
" I shall be glad to go into business with you."

" In the spring, then, we will do so. Now I
am over here, I mean to see something of Europe.

You must write to your uncle, stating the amount of the deficit. Give him a draft on Mr. Townsend, who is your aunt's executor, for the whole sum. Write to the executor yourself, also, directing him to take care of the balance till your return."

"I have about the value of thirty thousand dollars with me," I added, with a blush, as I thought of the means by which I had obtained it.

After this conference I felt more cheerful than for months before. I realized that Tom's earnest prayer for me had been heard, and that God had forgiven my great sin. I pledged myself anew to be faithful. I trembled when I thought that, if my aunt's dying bounty had not been interposed to save me, I might have spent a portion of my life in prison. Truly, I had every thing to be grateful for. When, after Tom and Bertha had retired, I told Lilian what had passed between my friend and myself, she wept tears of joy and gratitude.

My story is told. We travelled in Europe till the end of February, and then sailed from Cadiz to Havana, and thence proceeded to New Orleans. I wrote to my uncle, and sent him the requisite papers to adjust my accounts. He replied to me in a very good-natured strain, for to him crime undiscovered was no crime at all. I wrote to my mother, also. I could not wound her with the terrible truth, and therefore did not allude to the reasons for my leaving Boston.

When we got home, we were warmly welcomed by all our friends. I was regarded as a rich man, for a young one, and people were not disposed to ask hard questions. I do not think my mother was ever fully satisfied as to the reason of my leaving Boston so suddenly, but she did not press me for an explanation.

Tom and I went into business in the spring. After paying every dollar I owed, I had about forty thousand dollars. My partner put in twenty thousand dollars, and I the same. We are doing well, and both of us stand well in the community. Mr. Bristlebach is dead, and my uncle still keeps my secret.

I bought a house similar to the one I had occupied for so brief a period in Needham Street, and our home was all that peace, plenty and grateful hearts could make it.

I do not yet feel like an innocent man; I can never feel so. I shall regret and repent my sin to the end of my life. But I appreciate all my blessings, not the least of which is my wife, who has been my guardian angel since the day that her horror of my crime assured me of the reality of truth and goodness.

I am trying, by every means in my power, to atone for my error, for which a lifetime is no more than sufficient. I was not inclined to evil by nature or by education, and, I still feel that my crime was the legitimate result of LIVING TOO FAST.

9 783337 119195